seeking . . .

by

Gloria Hanson

2019

    A shorter version of the first portion of this book was previously published as a stand-alone novella, titled *Nighttime* as part of a collection entitled **Musings**, published in 2017 [EAN-13: 9781974- 402656]. To my surprise, many readers and friends asked, 'but what happens next?'
    It was a puzzlement. However, once I was settled in my new home on Cape Cod, inspiration struck. The first portion was slightly edited and lengthened, in order to more easily combine with the new second half.

Acknowledgements

Thanks to my daughter, Daria, who has read my books and continues to encourage and support.
I dedicate this book to her.

As always, Kelly Ferjutz, my friend, patient editor and role model deserves many thanks and much appreciation.

Other books by Gloria Hanson

The Life of An Ordinary Girl Living in Extraordinary Times

Late Night Stories

From Sevens to Seventies The Grand Girls Book of Poetry

A Long Way to Heaven: The Caretaker's Tale

Two Guys in America

Musings...A Sort of Memoir

List of Characters

Humans

Nicholas Zervas , 41, astronaut
NASA psychologist

Jane Halpern , 39. physician scientist
Partner to Nicholas

Gladys Henderson, 81, widow
Former biology teacher

Joan Dreyfus, 86, widow
Arthritic

Jordan Kennedy, 65,
retired Naval Officer

Ara Hamidi, 42, oncologist
Partner to Jordan

Donald Tracy , 59, widower
Bon Vivant

Vicky Simmons, 52, retired
Hospital Administrator

Joshua Lipman, 60, actor
Wealthy son

Ernest Hobart, 70, journalist
Retired

Charles Trainor, 76, lawyer
Mild dementia

Kate Trainor, 74, Buddhist
Wife and caretaker

Leia
child of Nicholas and Jane

Flavia
babysitter for Leia   Service Asst. Bot

Jeffrey Givens -   survivor on Planet Earth
Human Biologist

Gray Ones – Ymirians

Group of space travelers -
Technologists/designers

Joe   Leader of the Grays

Oden   Grays engineer/designer

Brown Ones   -   Ymirians

Group of space travelers -
Engineering types

Brown 1X   Leader of the Browns

Robot Categories

Service bots   white- topped on Ymir

Service Asst. bot   red/white striped staff

Recreation bots   red-trainers, teachers on Ymir

Medical bots   green-topped staff on Ymir

Handy bots   blue-topped staff on Ymir

Engineer bots   brown -topped on Ymir

Science bots   yellow-topped on Ymir

Military bots   silver-topped on Ymir

Explorer bots   striped brown and gray

seeking . . .

part one

Chapter 1
The Arrival of the Space Travelers

It was nighttime, and the sky was sparkling from stars easily discerned in the dark space, unencumbered by city lights. The arrivals looked in awe as they stepped out of the vehicle and onto the snow-covered ground. In the distance, they could see a dome shaped structure made of ice or what looked like ice. Narrow slits in the building let thin rays of light illuminate the darkness.

Nicholas, their guide, interrupted their silent wonder and urged them to trudge towards their new home away from home. As they came closer to the structure, they began to mumble and complain. They gaped in horror as they approached the door that opened into an elevator. Piling into the narrow cab lined with imported furs from earth, they saw that the labels were still hanging from each piece; and the riders read about the origin and the previous owner of the covering.

As the elevator began to move they realized that they were going down, not up as they had expected. They huddled close to each other or as close as they could get with the heavy space suits and headgear, and they searched for answers in their neighbors' faces. No information was forthcoming from their fellow travelers or their guide, a towering figure of a man accustomed to taking charge amid a group filled with apprehension and fear.

At the right time, he would speak through the microphone zipped into his plastic helmet and clarify their location in the structure and in the cosmos. Until then, he guided his sheep gently but firmly as they descended into the depths. The silence was frozen fear, and their passivity borne of knowing that there was no exit, no change of mind, no turning back.

The travelers, all retirees had embarked on an adventure to discover the effects of space travel and space residency on their health, – both physical and mental – and their social behavior. In their dream-like state, they envisioned a new version of an apartment building with ten suites, a patio, and a moon-like landscape. Now each one practiced the breathing and meditating exercises they had learned during their training.

Sometimes one could hear the rapid breathing and low moaning when their practice failed. It was difficult to continue breathing – it was easier to hold your breath and challenge your brain to tell you that this was not happening. You were dreaming this whole thing, and soon you would wake up and see the reality you had been led to believe. A few of them suspected that they had been given a hallucinogen, since they felt as if they were re-experiencing an LSD trip.

"Where are we going, Commander Nicholas?" one courageous traveler blurted out before realizing that his words were not going to register to the guide or to his fellow travelers.

"You will soon see. Don't worry. Stay calm – nothing to worry about – you will be okay."

That was the only sound heard for the next half hour or so. No one had any sense of time or distance now. It was as if they had passed into a space where time was unnecessary. Why bother?

Time on earth meant something, a phenomenon by which humans sense and record changes in their environment or in their perceptions of the universe. Of course, there was no absolute time, but they had anticipated being able to synchronize events and make sense of their reality.

There was no more certainty on this cold planet where they were descending to escape time and mass. They had hurtled through space to get here, and now were spiraling down into the unknown. They had assumed that their new location would be on the surface of a planet. No one had bothered to ask when they signed on, and now the descent unraveled their sense of place. Were they going to Hades?

The landing had been a soft one as landings go. It was not like the bumpy, scary descent on this planet where the ground appeared to want to come up through the space craft. This elevator landing was quiet and smooth, but it elicited a different kind of fear because they knew they were not on terra firma but below it. How far? Probably several hundred miles below the permafrost. It was a while before the large metal doors opened and revealed the site of their new home.

Looming above them was a tall building made of what looked like bricks with doors and windows resembling any apartment complex constructed in the 1920's by immigrant laborers on Planet Earth. The front door was made of some translucent material and wood or, at least, what looked like wood. Windows graced the front, sides and back of the building, and grass lawns and flower beds surrounded the lower level.

The crowd stood in awe as Nicholas directed them to exit the elevator. They were frozen in space and could not move. It was as if they were back on planet earth, back to their home and in their community. The light resembled sunshine, and clouds dotted the skyscape. There were roads leading to where? Sidewalks ending where? They looked around and worried and wondered about this destination.

Nicholas moved slowly and removed his bulky space suite, helmet and boots. He now looked like a regular earth guy with khaki trousers, a black tee and sneakers. They all looked at him as he breathed the air, smelled the flowers and strolled round the perimeter of the building. What were they to do? Obviously, he wanted them to do what he had done so effortlessly. He was not going to issue orders because he did not have to show his authority. All he had to do is behave as if he were back home, and he knew that his people would ultimately follow his lead. What else could they do? Stand in frozen terror forever?

Slowly and deliberately, one figure came forward from the crowd and began to disrobe. She piled her space suit, helmet and boots on top of Nicholas' apparel. Her name tag spelled out her last name – Henderson. Then she began to look at herself and examine her clothing; and as she checked herself, she recognized the jeans and blue blouse she had worn upon arrival at the space center. The gray hoodie covered her arms and shoulders but lay open revealing an eyeglass chain around her neck. The sneakers matched her sweater in color and looked brand new.

Her ears were pierced with small round gold earrings, and her watch stood out with a face too big for her delicate wrist. On her left hand, she wore a gold wedding ring and a gold, diamond-studded band that stood out on the long fingers of the heavily veined hand. Her hair was light ash brown, her eyes a stunning blue, and her facial skin was peachy and wrinkled. Her age, you ask. She was hovering around eighty years. She did not speak but began to move, following Nicholas as he walked around the structure.

One by one, the others followed her lead by shedding their space gear and piling it on top of the small mound. Silently, they wondered where the pile would end up – burned, discarded in space or maybe stored for their return flight to Planet Earth? Hoping for the latter, they added those thoughts to the ones they feared to ask. All they could do was wonder – wonder and hope for the promised outcome.

They now realized that they had been brainwashed by their government into thinking that this adventure was necessary for the health and welfare of American seniors and the future of the country. While there might have been a kernel of truth in the narratives, the officials failed to inform the travelers of the details of this journey into space.

John Glenn knew what he was getting into when he took a space ride in his seventy seventh year, but they did not. Of course, the seniors had been caught up in the excitement of the moment; here was a chance to travel, all expenses paid, to an exotic faraway place where they could stay awhile, explore and then return to Planet Earth and be swept up into the celebrity world and the possibility of making money from interviews and book deals. Watching television programs on rocket launching and the beautiful images of their planet romanticized the adventure.

Each one had made a bargain with the devil of uncertainty for a price. They had not shared their concerns with each other or family members. They had been individually targeted and encouraged to remain in their silos for security's sake. Each thought they had a special mission and they had been chosen because of their individual character traits that labeled them as special, unique and courageous.

Gladys Henderson, the first explorer, had been

a widow for five years. She had retired from teaching biology years before her husband had become ill. During those golden years, she volunteered, took yoga classes and lunched with her friends when she wasn't taking care of her mate. Following a turn for the worse, he became dependent on her caring and caretaking and expressed his need for her constant presence. Once he died, she took care of legal business, grieved for what seemed forever and returned to the bosom of her family and friends.

When Nicholas first appeared at her door, he introduced himself as a psychologist from NASA who was sent to interview her for a possible important mission. She looked at him in disbelief, but decided to listen to this crazy guy who came out of nowhere, but looked like the classic picture of a proper gentleman scientist.

They sat in her suite by the window that overlooked the front lawn of the building, 2000 South Park Boulevard in Hershey, Pennsylvania. He showed her some documents that explained the mission and then presented a power point description of the planet on his laptop, the space craft, the benefit analysis and the few risks. He described the goal of the study as helping senior earthlings understand the challenges of space travel and living on a planet away from home. What would the individual feel while in space and in an alien environment?

The traveler would be studied from a physiological, psychological and spiritual viewpoint, and all data would be available to the scientists. All earthly details such as displacement from community, daily tasks and social disengagement would be taken care of by the NASA team of social workers, accountants and psychologists. Nicholas would be in charge and would accompany her on the journey.

"Why not?" she reasoned, "I can be part of something bigger than myself and my little constrained world. I will be a cool eighty-two year old Grandma to my grandchildren who visit once a year." She became the first recruit.

The stage was set for Nicholas to enlist someone else for his team. Luckily, most of his choices already lived near each other in a condominium building on a corner street in Hershey. He knew general facts about all of them, including their different political orientations, and hoped that he could find some hooks that would make it easier for them to join. For his next big fish, he chose a retired Navy career guy who lived with his second wife in the condo near Gladys.

The two of them could possibly welcome an escape since neither his family or hers were too happy about this union. Coming from different religious traditions, he being a born-again Christian and she a Muslim, they sought to meld a union that could ignore the contradictory traditions in modern day America. Since he was retired and somewhat of a house husband while Ara Hamidi worked as an oncologist at the local hospital, they could co-exist and find solace in each other's company, despite the twenty-year age difference.

Once they had settled on the trip as a temporary escape from the stressors of their families, they were eager to set off on the big adventure. Here it was – a geographic cure that would give them and their parents, siblings, children, cousins, aunts, uncles and religious advisors relief.

Jordan Kennedy, Executive Officer-Retired at sixty-five was balding and stiff jawed. having been on board many different vessels, he would bring experience and management of day-to-day activities and fill in for Nicholas should he need to be absent on any stage of the mission. Of course, there was a downside of a recruit having any kind of power and being second in command. Nicholas decided to have an assistant who would take the lead and keep the Executive Officer in his place.

The presence of a doctor on the mission was an added plus. Granted, Ara Hamidi at forty-two years, was an oncologist, but she could also pinch hit as a general physician in the event of any minor medical problems. She had come around to the idea of this trip as an adventure and as a way for her to leave the messiness of her family's strict Muslim faith. She was also a beautiful woman with olive skin and straight black hair surrounding a roundish face with bewitching brown eyes.

He caught his wandering mind and then thought of someone who could be both assistant and medical officer. Jane Halpern would fit the bill, and he believed she would be more than happy to accompany him since she had expressed a romantic interest in him. She could be an answer to many of his issues surrounding this mission and his personal life. She was a tall woman with blondish hair and piercing blue eyes. Not only was she attractive but she had been trained as an MD/PHD physician scientist, an older woman of 39 years who had never married but carried herself with poise and dignity and did not hesitate to maintain the chain of command.

She might have been intimidated by another potential recruit, Vicky Simmons, who was at fifty-two an early retiree from hospital administration. Ebullient and blonde, she was a hazel-eyed gal who had divorced five years ago, but was sweet and still attracted to the opposite sex. The word on the street was that however sugary she could be, she could also unleash a string of invectives and gossip with the best of the men and women she befriended. She had decided that a trip in space was what she needed now that she was single and determined to bring some excitement to her life following her divorce from an abusive husband. Being an organized individual, she certainly could assist in maintaining order on the mission yet hopefully accept Jane's leadership.

Perhaps the retired widower and bon vivant, Donald Tracey, could also keep her in line by offering nightly libations and a way to vent any frustrations she might have with Nicholas or any of the other travelers. Both were from Irish ancestry, but he was a quiet sort with a ready quip and a seemingly good listening ear – when he did hear conversations. Averse to wearing a hearing aid, he could rely on Vicky to translate. They lived on the same floor of the condominium building and had been friendly for three years. Having taken care of his wife who slowly deteriorated battling Parkinson's Disease, he longed for an escape from familiar places and people. Nicholas thought that the Vicky and Donald alliance was a useful combination made in heaven. He might be wrong about all these alliances, but he prided himself on having a good sense of people and their foibles.

The aging actor from a wealthy family had been a little more difficult to pigeon-hole because of his profession. He might reject the trip because of theatrical commitments, but Nicholas thought he could convince him on the basis of his current rocky relationship with a fellow thespian who had made it clear that she did not want to be the fourth Mrs. Lipman.

Nicholas was convinced that he could convince Joshua Lipman, a handsome, sixty-year-old year old, white-hired leading man to join if he could be made to see how this voyage would give him good press for his acting career and make the heart grow fonder for his current hard-to-get sweetheart. His family had supported his trip in thinking that the time away in space would help him personally and in a profession that had been stuck in neutral on Planet Earth.

Nicholas had been correct, and Joshua had

consented to the trip with the understanding that he could entertain his neighbors with his dramatic renditions. Nicholas viewed his importance as a candidate for a memory study focusing on brain changes during space flight. In addition, Joshua had undergone heart valve surgery the previous year making him a good subject for linking cardiovascular disease and lifestyle changes in a new environment.

There had been another hard sell in the personage of an older, patrician corporate lawyer, Charles Trainor, a stooped over seventy-six year old male, suffered from a slowing gait, early dementia, poor hearing and a penchant for living by his own rules when in a politically diversified group. He was the most fragile member of this group.

Perhaps his wife, Kate Trainor, could keep an eye on her aging husband and help him play by the rules. It would be interesting to observe how space travel, and a new–and different– controlled environment would affect the dementia and the relationship between the husband and wife since she had an outwardly global view of the world in the Buddhist tradition of spirituality.

She was a post-menopausal woman of seventy-four who had been a massotherapist and could be a perfect candidate for the effect of space travel on muscle function. Her ability to communicate with all of the neighbors in her building would allow her to become the moral arbitrator and peace maker. The couple had been enthralled with the idea of space travel as their great last adventure.

And there would have had to be a group peacemaker if the two remaining seniors decided to join. Joan Dreyfus, the eighty-six year old widow with poor ambulatory skills was a critical mistress who "kissed up and kicked down." She could become a problem if she could not get along with others due to her arthritic pain and sharp tongue, but her age and opinions might add some spice to the group. In addition, she was a perfect patient to assess the effects of gravity changes and space travel on her psoriatic arthritis.

She and Ernest Hobart would make a marvelous pair of old curmudgeons. What would happen to the cranky former journalist who had a reputation of selfishness and misogyny and Joan, the widow, who was sixteen years younger, but appeared to look a decade older than he actually was? His publisher had encouraged him to take this trip and write about it. He had reluctantly agreed.

Would space travel and a new habitat change his outlook on life? Would the new life influence his personality and brain function?

Nicholas looked out on the screen in the module, remembering the difficulty of cohort selection, but now he congratulated himself with the variety of individuals he had chosen, the melding of social science, psychological and medical research studies that would produce data he could mine to propel him to the upper echelons of space scientists.

He thought again about the space scientist and physician, Jane Halpern, who was a competent, no-nonsense woman with a bag full of social skills. She could not only design experiments but would keep him in line. He had been told by his commanding officer that she was the perfect second in command, or even the first to lead this motley group and bring balance to the overly confident man in charge.

He and Jane would be sharing a suite built on the first floor with a command center living room and 2 bedrooms and a bath. He thought to himself, "Would they really need two bedrooms?"

He drifted out of his fantasy and returned to reality and to the enormous task before him.
He and his team would complete this mission within a few years and return to Earth with a parade down Fifth Avenue. What could go wrong?

Chapter 2
Is this for real?

Lights went on in the structure as they approached it, and Nicholas beckoned his team to follow him through the front door and into a gracious looking entry hall with couches covered in damask and comfortable-looking upholstered chairs in groups of four. Round coffee tables held bowls of yellow miniature chrysanthemums that peered out from a mixture of pebbles and grainy, gray growth-factor soil. Were these flowers the real thing or were they silken replicas brought from Planet Earth? There were no plant carcasses around to indicate life, but one could never be sure that a fallen yellowing leaf had been spun from silk.

The colors in the room were in shades of gold and muted brown. The floors had been buffed to reveal oak-like slats that showed off the rich hues of the oriental rugs. The chandelier lighting was subdued and glowed to make everyone look younger and rosier. A buzzer system was hung discretely in the corner, and Gladys noticed that the names of her fellow travelers were printed in a list alongside of a number to press to gain entrance. The familiar sound of Mozart played softly in the background.

"Who did all this?" asked Jordan as he scoped out the entryway and pulled Ara closer to him. He was waiting for an army of aliens to appear to answer his question since Nicholas did not appear to be interested in dispelling shock and awe.

"All in due time. Let's get to our new apartments, rest, and tomorrow, Nicholas will answer all questions. I am sure you are exhausted," Jane explained as she eagerly tried to protect her Commander.

"There is some chamomile tea in your kitchen pantry and a bottle of Ambien to help you if you are having trouble falling to sleep so let's go," Nicholas chimed in with his straightforward approach to shepherding his flock. "Look around and make yourselves at home, grab a snack and get some rest. We have a big day tomorrow."

He opened another door to an inner hallway that contained steps and a small elevator. Since they all couldn't fit into the small cab, he called out names for each floor and led the occupants to each floor. Nicholas dropped off the occupants on floor 2: Gladys in one apartment at one end and Jordan and Ara in the other. He opened their doors and asked Jane to show them around.

He then left to lift the third-floor residents, Charles and Kate and Joshua, to their new abodes. Repeating his second-floor routine, he waited for Jane and went downstairs again to get Joan and Ernest up to the fourth floor. He was somewhat gentle with Joan since she seemed shaky and hesitant, but he relinquished control to Jane when she arrived to rescue him once again.

He returned to the inner hall and whisked Donald and Vicky into their respective units. Checking his phone, he waited for Jane to appear. They took their time making sure there were no incidents or major loud complaints from their charges and retired to their apartment on the adjoining street. It had its own private entrance. Silence, privacy and relief.

"I find it difficult to believe that it has gone this well. I was expecting a mutiny and a demand to turn around and return to Earth. How do you feel about the group? Any regrets?" Jane asked once they had settled down and lit up a joint.

"I'll make it work with your help. We can't tell now if they will adjust, crash or demand a trip home. They seem quite enthralled with the trip so far, but I know they'll want more details and guidance. It is a good cohort ranging in age, history, physical and mental health and intelligence. Before we retire, let's go over the drill for tomorrow."

"Business first, huh? You certainly are a control freak, but as of tonight you are in charge. Then we shall see."

Before turning in for the night, Nicholas had scheduling homework. He went to the screen on the desk in his small study room and typed in the date and time for the cleaning robot team to leave their posts and roll through the common areas to vacuum and dust. They would commence their duties now and be done in an hour. Quietly their twelve-inch silver little forms would begin to whirl and twirl while extending their long mechanical arms to reach over the furniture. The sound was one of a soft hum and the smell one of a floral fragrance cloud. When done, they rolled over to the closet closest to the back door and piled one upon the other in precise moves and began to wind down. Eight little robots stacked themselves ever so neatly into the dock and recharged themselves ready to serve their master Nicholas whenever he decided to program them for other tasks.

Vicky had taken a shower in her luxurious tub/shower combo on floor 1 and sat on her bed to finish drying her hair when she heard the soft hum outside her door. Curiosity was not going to kill this cat. She would not be opening her door to investigate. She had been courageous enough for one day, one week, one year or however long it took them to travel to this outpost. She could wait for the Commander's explanation; and any way she suddenly felt very tired, and despite the wet hair, she lay down on the pillow and fell into a peaceful sleep.

Hearing the silence and the click of the drones in the dock, Nicholas began the next programming task for his little helpers. Planning a buffet dinner for his team of travelers, he needed the kitchen drones to set up the serving areas, along with five round tables with dishes, glasses and silverware, flower centerpiece and name cards.

What can't these babies of artificial intelligence do? Their chef and cook counterparts could cook and serve but were not programmed to do the menial tasks of set up and clean up.

"What a world we have lived in for the past decade. Before then, a guy would have had to hire a catering company to cook, prepare, serve and clean up or marry a woman who could accomplish all of that good stuff," Nicholas thought.

"Jane, I am done working and ready for some rest and relaxation. How about you?,"

"I am ready for you, Commander Nicholas," the passionate Jane. chuckled.

Chapter 3
The Dwellings and the Dwellers

Jordan and Ara took their time exploring their apartment. He held her hand and forged ahead as a gentlemanly military man was taught to do. The lights turned on automatically as they made their way down the hall. Kitchen, dining room, laundry room, two bedrooms, living room and two bathrooms had been meticulously decorated to match their apartments on earth.

"How did they know what our apartment looked like, Jordan? This is eerie. I don't recall any visits there from Nicholas or Jane," whispered Ara as she moved closer to Jason and tightly held onto his arm.

"They probably hacked into the security system on my phone when we were away and made some kind of file they could refer to. Privacy is a thing of the past, my dear. Big Brother is always watching or can always tune in when they want," Jordan answered trying to remain calm and sound like the brave male who would protect his little flower.

"I don't like this so far. I feel as if we are in a sci-fi movie. I keep waiting for aliens to appear," Ara said as she began to breathe deeply when she was inhaling, stopping and holding her breath until she could no longer continue the rhythm.

"Let's check out the refrigerator. I am starving," Jordan responded as he led his trembling beloved into the kitchen.

When they opened the door of the large stainless steel appliance, they stood back in amazement.

"I'll be damned. They even know what we like to eat! Let's not waste any time. They might come in and haul us out to an assignment," Jordan joked as he pulled out pizza boxes, yoghurt cups, salad bowls and dressing.

The lights in the apartment across the walkway were also lit, and they could see Gladys wandering around checking out the pantry and the refrigerator. She looked as if she were in a daze and could be seen opening and closing her mouth as if she were speaking to someone. Actually, Gladys had been talking to someone as she always checked everything out with her late husband; and in this way, she re-assured herself that her words had meaning for her actions. She took out a sandwich from the refrigerator, opened a bottle of water and sat down to eat. She could not taste much these days so it did not matter to her if it was baloney and cheese or roasted veggies on a bun. They tasted more or less the same but satisfied the need to fuel up.

She waved at her neighbors and tried to open the back door so she could speak to them about the goings on, but she found that the door was locked with no key in sight.

"Well, it's probably better that way," she thought to herself as she tidied up and retreated to the bedroom.

All of the tired travelers soon gave up their explorations; and, following a cursory examination of their quarters, they indulged in a bit of food and libation. They knew that they had arrived at their destination; and although all of their living spaces looked like the ones they had had at home, they thought that this was some kind of mirage, some kind of digital reproduction. There was nothing to be done so they resorted to a Zen-like state and lived in the moment until they gave in to an overwhelming desire to lie down and sleep. It was as if someone had put a spell on the space travelers.

Lights went out for all the common areas; and followed by clicks of the door locks, the building fell into silence – a stillness that was akin to an underwater garden. Fish swam without making waves, starfish, eels, sting rays shimmied above the sand without sound. The music had stopped, and everything and everyone was in place.

Outside and on the surface, figures draped in brown circled the landing area and the elevator structure. These creatures were glacially silent, going about their business with quiet determination. They held no weapons and appeared curious but not ferocious or menacing. They peered, paused and planted their bodies around the strange objects as if they had knocked on the door and were awaiting an invite. There did not appear to be a leader, but they seemed to act in unison as if they were all connected by some invisible cord. Nicholas and Jane watched on their security camera image screen as the spectral figures floated around the upper layer to inspect the scene. Then without warning, the "Brown Ones" receded out of focus.

The sleeping humans had not been seen by the night visitors due to the fact that they were far below the surface safely hidden from any visiting eyes or scanners. For now, their presence was a mystery to the scouting team of brown shadow-like figures. Nicholas and Jane, having convinced themselves that these creatures carried no visible weapons, watched in awe wondering about the visitors. Were they sentient beings? Were they part of a bad dream that would be gone upon awakening? Watch and wonder. Time would tell.

Chapter 4
Settling In

A very special lunch had been prepared for the travelers. As they made their way into the dining area, they were surprised to see the elegant settings at the tables. Every detail had been executed. Plates, silverware and glasses sat in perfect harmony. Centerpieces on each table held a small vase of flowers that floated up and down on a base. How, they wondered, had Nicholas done all this? Did he and Jane stay up all night to prepare? Did they cook, too? They could not imagine a caterer being down in this part of town. They found their place cards, sat down at their designated places and waited while listening to a Mozart piano concerto piped in from a small round object attached to the ceiling. They did not chat with their table mates, but when Nicholas and Jane appeared, the travelers stood and applauded them. Why? Apparently, they thought that he and Jane had arranged the tables and settings.

Nicholas and Jane smiled, and they went to a table set out for them. Nicholas began to speak, "Good afternoon, fellow adventurers, and welcome to the new home of 'Team Earth Explorers.'

We will enjoy a fine lunch prepared by our staff, and following that repast, I will tell you more about your new locale and what is in store for you. Enjoy your meal and relax."

As soon as he finished his short monologue, he pointed to the swinging doors at the rear of the room. The tall mahogany-looking doors opened, and out came rows of robots bearing dishes on their long arms. Their spindly legs and oval mechanical faces gave them the look of robots the earthlings had seen in adventure and space movies they had attended with their grandchildren. The bots placed the dishes on a long table at the front of the room and proceeded to transfer the food onto warming trays. They pulled out silver-looking serving spoons and forks, and in a graceful twirl, they rolled into what must have been a kitchen where they could be heard whirling around and tinkering with glassware.

"Please come up and help yourselves," Jane exclaimed in a voice that sounded like a hostess in a restaurant. She could see that the motionless guests would need a nudge.

What followed was a moment of silence followed by a slow walk to the serving table. The earthlings picked up their plates and obediently spooned the food onto the white dinner dishes. There was a tray with what looked like roast beef, another with salmon, and one with roasted vegetables and pasta. Baskets of warm rolls graced the end of the table near the bowl of spring mix salad laced with tiny tomatoes and cucumber slices.

Returning to their seats, they commenced to eat the meal, but they remained silent and stone-faced – until they looked up to hear the door opening and the robot troop crawl out with water and what looked like wine bottles to fill the glasses of their guests. None of them had ever been so near a robot. In fact, none of them even owned a Rumba-style vacuum that had become so popular with the technologically inclined. Jaws dropped and eyes lowered as the travelers swallowed hard and tried not to look vacant and dumbfounded.

"My friends from planet Earth, I welcome you to Ymir or planet Gliese 581b. We are about 119 trillion miles or 20.37 light years from our original home. This planet outside our solar system was chosen because astronomers thought, incorrectly, I might add, that it was most like earth. Our space crafts discovered that it faced its star so it was in permanent day while the other side, they thought, faced away from the star and is in permanent night. We are on the day side, and we sit on a rocky surface made mostly of silicate. We recently discovered that the surface was pockmarked with gigantic holes in the ground – holes that went deep towards the center. One of these provided us with the ability to build the metropolis we are now inhabiting. This has enabled us to create an earth-like metropolis. "

"Getting back to the planet – it revolves, but its day side always faces its star or sun, the red dwarf star, Gliese 581 in the Lunar galaxy. The surface is icy cold, even on the day side; and as far as we know, there is no life as we know it here. The name given by the astronomers who first saw it was Ymir, from Norse mythology meaning that it is said was born of an icy river."

"What do you mean by metropolis, Nicholas?" asked Charles Trainor as he tried to be calm when he heard the word "metropolis."

The others muttered and whispered to each other since they had been thinking the same thing. There was one astonishing and surprising thing after another. How much could an aging body and mind absorb in one day?

"Yes, metropolis. You have seen only part of our underground world, but you will get a tour tomorrow morning. Get ready for some pretty spectacular sights. We have all of the businesses you had in your neighborhood, nearby cultural institutions and malls for shopping. The only luxury we don't have is the gasoline engine automobile or self-driving cars. You will be driven around by our drivers, and I don't think you would be surprised to hear that snazzy robots will be your guides tomorrow and later when you need to get some groceries."

Gladys seemed unfazed as she sat up in her chair and asked, "Speaking of groceries, where does the food come from?"

"Ah, Gladys, good question. Right now, the food has been brought from earth by a private company, Planet Express, that launches its payloads to distant galaxies. The food was picked fresh and frozen or slaughtered and frozen to insure food safety. In the second phase of our plan we are beginning to construct large green houses for the vegetables and fruits. Until we figure out how to house cows, chickens, pigs and lambs, or else maybe biologically clone some and grow them here, we will continue to import."

"That could take years, Nicholas. We are here only for a year or two. I have to get back to Earth for my granddaughter's wedding," Gladys responded with a worried look and a snarky tone.

"Well, let's wait and see. All will be revealed in good time, Gladys. Meanwhile, let's give a hand to the Service Robots who provided this delicious meal." The Earthlings clapped but thought how ridiculous it was to applaud machines.

Jane leapt at the chance to invite the surprised humans, "When we have eaten our meal, let's take a little walk around this compound to acquaint you with its major features."

Following a delicious apple pie and ice cream desert, the sated travelers followed Nicholas and Jane out the front door of the building and fell into line as they made their way along a cement sidewalk encircling the apartment complex. As they walked they thought they saw a parkland setting surrounding them. Trees, grass, plantings of hydrangeas, rose bushes, forsythia among other species spread out before them. Looking upward, they could see a blue sky dotted with cirrus clouds, as a warm breeze enveloped them. They tried to bend to touch the flowers, but were surprised to observe the retreat of the plant into the ground. It became obvious that the environment was to be seen but not touched, experienced by the mind but not the body. This picture was a mirage similar to those they had seen in old movies of desert travelers searching for oases and water. The older travelers wondered whether this was the virtual reality their grandchildren inhabited while on their electronic gadgets.

Kate, who loved to hike and enjoy the beauty of nature asked, "Can we walk in that park, Nicholas? And where does it go?"

"You certainly can use that path anytime. It leads into town where we'll be visiting tomorrow."

"Perhaps some of us could hike there and meet up with the those who prefer to be driven. What do you think, Nickolas?" Jane chimed in as she attempted to detour the direction of the conversation

"I think it is best that we stay together on this first excursion," Nicholas responded in a firm tone.

"Why?" Kate responded, "Are wild animals in the woods, aliens or other scary things?"

"No, no, nothing like that, but I want all my cats to share the same experiences before I set you loose. Furthermore, you might get lost," Nicholas said firmly and authoritatively as he needed his cohort to remain where he could observe and keep an eye on them while he conducted his research.

These first few days had to set the course, while they were still in awe and too scared to rebel or to wander. He understood that this could change in the blink of an eye, and he did not want a mutiny of senior citizens on his watch.

Chapter 5
The Metropolis

The next morning at 9AM sharp –Earth time, Nicholas gathered his people in front of the apartment complex as a driverless minibus pulled up to the curb. The door opened, and everyone stepped in and naturally looked for their seat belts. None could be found, and they once again they began to wonder what was in store for them.

Sitting in the front passenger seat, Nicholas tapped his phone, and the van began to move and steer itself down a narrow road leading to town. Nicholas began to point out the landmarks, describing each in great detail for he knew all of the trees, streams, and low-lying structures along the way. It appeared that the domed buildings were designated as future greenhouses or storage facilities.

As they approached the "town" a Main Street appeared – a roadway with storefronts on each side including a beauty salon, barbershop, coffee and pizza shops, clothing stores, a Mid-Donald's with its chartreuse yellow arches straddling the front door, and, finally, a building that looked like a grocery store and a pharmacy. At the end of the businesses, a flat-roofed, rectangular building spread out on a grassy parkland.

"That, my dear passengers,"" said Nicholas as he pointed to the structure, "is the community center where you can go to dance, exercise, take classes and play tennis, ping pong or paddle ball."

"Who manages it? Teaches classes? Who will tell us where things are?" Joshua asked as he strained to get a closer look at the facility.

"You can guess, can't you? It won't be me, I assure you," Nicholas responded with a note of brash humor.

"You mean robots?" Joan piped up.

"Yes, of course, and you will get to know them by color as they will be a group of Recreation Robots. They will give you the tour, show you the facilities, turn on the videos to lead you in Yoga, Zumba, Pilates or coach you on how to lift weights or learn how to play bridge. Isn't this exciting?"

"Nicholas, are you, Jane and us the only humans on this planet?" Joan asked in an exasperated tone.

"As far as we know."

"That's reassuring, and if we don't get along, we don't have any options – we're stuck with you and the rest of us," she continued, as she began to understand the nature of this grand experiment. "I hope this doesn't play out as a *1984* for seniors."

Everyone chuckled, but underneath the humor lay an uneasiness about the future of their mission, their safety and their return to Planet Earth. How much of the sales pitch had been exaggeration and untruths? What and whom could they believe? Were the words mirroring the unreality of this place?

"Now, now, roll with the punches, guys. There is nothing nefarious in this mission. You were not sold a bill of goods. As you were told, you are here as part of our research team designed to explore space travel and extraterrestrial life's effects on older Planet Earth citizens. You are not meant to be here forever – two years at the most, and you will go home if you wish."

"I wish I were home right now," exclaimed Joan in one final attempt to remain calm and collected.

"How do we get around, Commander?" Jordan asked in his familiar military tone, turning to formally address both Nicholas and the crowd.

"You can walk or take the van as long as you instruct the robots as to the time of pickup and return. It's like having your own driver on a schedule."

"And how do we shop? Do you also issue credit cards or give us a cash allowance?" Jordan continued. "You know that the devil is in the details."

"Good question. You will be issued a credit card and an identity pin that you wear whenever you go out and about."

"And it has a GPSS so you always know where we are – day and night? Gladys queried in partial jest.

"Gladys, you hit the nail on the head," Nicholas responded trying to use phrases that corresponded to her age and historical period.

"So, you always know what is going on with us no matter where we are or what we are doing?" Jordan asked in an exasperated voice.

"Well, most of the time, but when you are safely tucked in at night, you can remove your pin and do what you wish. Does that allay your concerns?"

"Tucked in? You mean locked in, don't you?" Ernest Hobart asked provocatively.

"I guess you could frame it in that way, Mr. Hobart, if you wish to put a negative spin on this security measure designed to keep you all safe."

"That's good enough for me, Chief, I want us all to be as secure as we can be," Kate Trainor chimed in as she tried to defuse conflict between Nicholas and the cranky Ernest.

Nicholas turned his head forward and began to act as guide again as he pointed out the swimming pool, tennis courts and walking paths on the way back to their compound. Nearing the apartment building, Nicholas pointed out a low structure close to their "home" where signs for hospital and emergency entrance grabbed the attention of the passengers.

"This is the clinic, hospital and ER where you are free to go anytime, day or night. It is free as are any prescription drugs you might need."

Gladys chuckled and speaking in a loud, comedian-like voice as she doubled over in laughter,

"And the staff is........? I guess Medical Robots reduce the cost of health care here. We might bring some back to Earth to help keep the baby boomers healthy."

The riders laughed out loud and began to point out familiar features in the surroundings. Overwhelmed with the sights, sounds and technology, they let down their guard and surrendered to their new reality.

"Let's hope that there are no more surprises today because my heart can't take more, exclaimed the diminutive Joan.

"I agree, Joan. All of this excitement and novelty have made me long for my old rocking chair and TV," Ernest replied.

"You will be there soon enough. Meanwhile let's enjoy these moments and be grateful for our intrepid leaders and the beauty of our make believe surroundings," Kate spoke with a trembling voice and pastor-like tone.

"Amen." The humans bowed their heads and spoke in unison.

Chapter 6
Managing the Place

Having heard that their apartment building would have to be managed by the residents, the Earthlings assembled and chose a Board of Managers composed of five members. This Board would abide by the bylaws set up by Nicholas and NASA management staff and manage the everyday affairs of the building. If anything needed repair, they would consult with the Handy-robot team to make sure it was done in a timely fashion. If the owners needed more lights in the common areas, the Board would order the fixtures from the hardware store in town.

In addition to these mundane tasks, the Board would call monthly meetings with the other owners to discuss the various aspects of living in a distant world. Some of the time, Nicholas or Jane would be present, but other times, they would meet only with their fellow travelers – or at least that was what they thought.

At one of their meetings, the topic was the inefficiency of the food staff. The Board president, Jordan Kennedy, led off the discussion.

"The Board has been receiving complaints from some of the owners that the food situation needs to be improved. Anyone interested in sharing your thoughts."

"I am getting tired of the same old menu for breakfast, lunch and dinner. I also want my dinner fixings to be brought earlier so that I can cook it early. Instead of the delivery being at 4PM, couldn't they drop it off at 2PM so I can put everything in the oven. Or could they deliver it prepared at 4PM? That way I can watch a movie or catch what passes as news following my meal and still be able to retire at 9PM," Joan Dreyfus offered. She had been waiting for this opportunity to express her concerns since the time of her arrival on Ymir.

"I'm satisfied with the delivery time and the quality of the food. After all we haven't started to grow things here yet; and until we have our own food supply, we should be happy with what we have," Gladys responded in a provocative tone. Gladys was not a fan of Joan's as she thought the woman was always complaining about something.

"What does everyone else think about this topic?" Jordan intervened as he was aware of the personal animosity of these two elders.

"I'm okay with the delivery time and the food because I have my cocktail hour around 5, and then everything tastes good after that," Donald responded mischievously because he knew that the only alcoholic beverage was a rye beer fermented and brewed in a tall building near town.

"Yuck," Joshua exclaimed, "I am hoping for a

vineyard inside one of those domed huts so I can get my wine. It can't come anytime soon."

"Dream on there, buddy," Ernest responded as he expounded on the necessary environmental requirements for making a fine wine.

"I would vote for a good brewery because I'm with Donald. The food always tastes better after a few beers," Vicky said, smiling and winking at Donald.

"I don't care if the delivery is made late or early," Charles responded, "because even though Kate spices up the food, I can't taste or smell much."

"I really don't know why several deliveries couldn't be made at different times. For God's sake, the drivers are robots. They don't have to finish early to go home to their little robots," Joan re-stated her entitlement position.

"I will note your comments and bring it up with Nicholas. He could not make it here today since he and Jane had to check something out on the surface. I saw them getting into the elevator when I was jogging," Jordan said as he attempted to bring this meeting to closure. He moved on and asked:

"How are we all doing these days? Missing home? What is going on?"

"I don't miss home because I was alone there and have more to do and think of here on this planet. I sleep better and have resigned myself to going with the flow. Sometimes I wonder if I will ever go back home to Planet Earth. I could die here. I wonder what they would do with my body," Joan answered as she averted her eyes from the group and stared into space.

"Hmm, I never even thought of that," Ernest answered with a grin, "The Funeral robot team would probably take us up on the elevator and dump us somewhere on the surface where we would remain frozen until some other earthlings visit."

"You know, Ernest, your remarks make my skin crawl. Not funny! Keep these outlandish thoughts to yourself. Wondering what will happen to me when I'm gone is not something I want to think about, especially when I am so far from home and my family. I'm feeling anxious enough without your dark humor," Gladys responded with an edge to her voice

Ernest did not apologize but gave her a disdainful look.

"I'm with you, Gladys, I'm having trouble adjusting to the now. All of this technical stuff running around gets my head spinning. I wouldn't give a damn if all those robots left and some humans took their places," Donald responded as he shook his head in dismay.

"That's not going to happen. Remember that Nicholas told us that we are probably the only humans in this God forsaken place. We have to make the best of it and befriend those little robots so they don't turn against us," Vicky said as she tried to steer the conversation to the positive.

"It sounds like we are all trying to deal with

our feelings with humor," Ara, who rarely spoke, told her neighbors. "I, for one, fear what is to come. I find it difficult to believe we are the only beings on this planet. I just hope they don't take the elevator and come down to our community."

"So, what would we do if there were aliens who visited? Shoot them? We don't have guns. We wouldn't know how to communicate since we don't know their language. We would have to become Amy Adams in the movie, *Arrival* and try to get them to leave. Or we could offer one of us as hostage," Donald joked.

"We probably will have killed each other before any aliens come to visit," Charles responded in kind.

"Well, this is getting macabre. Let's end this meeting now," President Jordan concluded.

Charles interjected with obvious glee, "Oh, just when it was just beginning to get interesting!"

Chapter 7
Getting More History

Nicholas called the general weekly meeting to order and proceeded to inform his subjects about the environment down under.

"Water for us comes from a natural aquifer found by early probes. It is frozen, of course, but it is easily converted to liquid, tested and made available via a system of natural aqueducts below our floors. It reminds me of the Roman ones except these are exposed by Robot engineers."

"Who built this place? Where did the materials come from? When was it started? Finished?" Gladys had been getting all worked up and waiting to unload the basket of questions she had been pondering since her arrival.

"Let's start with the last question first," Nicholas responded in a very patient manner as he attempted to slow things down. "This project began in the era of Sputnik although it was a secret endeavor planned by an international team of scientists.

It was something like the planning for the development of America's atomic bomb. Keeping it a secret was very important because of the political atmosphere at the time, especially between the

United States and Russia."

Jane interrupted and added, "Well, who found this place? Of all the planets in the universe, what made NASA choose this one, you ask?"

"The astronauts who went to the moon and then later to Mars were able to locate a stable planet that was similar to earth and did not rotate on its own axis and around a sun. They located Ymir and its star and decided this was the place that could serve as an outpost for our explorations of space and future homes because planet Earth was showing signs of deterioration and of possible destruction by asteroids or even human mischief."

"So, we are the advance team that will serve as guinea pigs for future generations," Donald stated in a matter of fact way as he stared at Nicholas with a facial expression showing both fear and disdain.

Nicholas avoided Donald's glance and continued, "In many ways, you are the future, but we will talk about that later. Now let me tell you how we built this facility. The Mars team discovered a substance on Mars that could be broken down into its basic atomic structure, transported and reassembled light years away.

That material, let's call it *plastiforon*, was then collected and beamed to this planet and reassembled by the Robot engineers according to the designs drawn by the famous architect/designers, Jesse Gortz and Frank Gelding. The robots had been programmed by teams at

NASA and sent to Ymir. These telerobots located the present site and completed the building three years ago – earth time."

"I guess the building is the easy part," Ernest responded, "but how did they bring the food that we have been eating? I didn't see any greenhouses down here, and the surface looks too cold and inhospitable for farming."

"Yes, you are right. Food has been transported here in a freeze-dried state, stored, defrosted when needed and made available to our culinary team of chef robots who themselves have been programmed by some famous chefs on Planet Earth. We do have plans, however, to build large greenhouses so we can grow our own food since we have developed a soil substitute and imported hardy seeds from earth," Nicholas continued.

"And how about the meat? Will you grow cows and pigs here to roam around the plantation?" Gladys questioned.

"Gladys, good question. We do have cloning facilities where our Robot Scientists are trying to get our own *Dolly* to get us started to develop our own breeds."

"*Oh, I see where this* is going to go – we're going to be cloned, too," Gladys burst forth with glee and horror as her neighbors looked to the astonished Nicholas for an answer.

Nicholas hesitated as he tried to fashion a response that was factual yet truthful, "Gladys, you should be cloned! There is no need to fret. We are nowhere near the point where we will ask for you to give us a saliva sample or stem cells so we can clone each one of you."

"Nowhere near that point? What in the hell does that mean, Nicholas?" Charles responded in a courtroom voice.

"Yes, it sounded as if you and your handlers have those plans in mind," Kate confirmed her husband's words.

A silence filled that room, and Nicholas tried to iron out the wrinkles in his thoughts. "Let me tell you that in case of a calamity on Planet Earth necessitating a longer stay on Ymir, scientists think that we may indeed have to clone the population we have in order to save the species."

"Calamity? Clone us to save the species? We are mostly old and full of mutations. Why would you want to clone us?" Gladys responded demonstrating that she remembered some of her Biology lessons.

"Scientists on Earth have developed techniques such as Crispit to out those bad genes." Nicholas had been trying to calm the crowd. He did not want to risk a mutiny or frantic messages to family and friends who would then sound the alarm and distort the message and perhaps abort the mission.

"Let's put this topic on the shelf for now and return to our discussion of the history of our goals and our facility. Do you have any more questions about this place, its history and the plans for the future?"

"Nicholas, perhaps you can put things on a

back shelf, but most of us can't do that so easily. I, for one, thought this was going to be a short space trip, and I could return to Earth and regale my grandchildren with exciting tales about Grandpa's adventures. Now I find that there is a good chance we won't be going back to Earth ourselves, but someone like ourselves might," Donald exclaimed with a groan and a heavy sigh.

"Yikes," Vicky shouts, "I thought I would become famous and find myself a handsome astronaut husband when I returned home. Instead I may return as a wilted lady with little hope of success."

"Are there any benefits to this mission? I mean personal ones, not idealistic statements of benefitting or saving mankind or the species?" Ernest asked.

"Do you ever think of anyone but yourself, Ernie? Maybe we have to take another look at this project and this place and find a new, or different meaning," Joan added from her point of view.

"Joan, you're much older so being marooned here doesn't have the same impact that it does to those of us who are younger and hopeful for a long life," Ernest responded in kind to the rebuke from his neighbor.

All of a sudden, an alarm rang out from the kitchen, and all conversation stopped, and everyone ran outside the building and huddled around the mulberry tree that had graced the area near the front door. "Saved by the bell," Nicholas muttered under his breath, "or more than likely by Jane."

Chapter 8
A Sighting

A siren rang out in the middle of the night awakening everyone. Jordan ran out of his unit and saw a strange sight. All of the robot teams were spinning around in the front hall and forming lines in front of the door. Each displayed a long barrel protruding out of the frontal section and pointed out to the door.

The humming sounds were becoming louder and more warlike until Nicholas appeared and held a computer-like device designed to calm a crowd. The teams stopped spinning and humming and became stone silent.

The scene soon became more crowded as the residents rose out of their beds and scurried down to see what was going on. Joan wearily joined the crowd of her neighbors and stared blankly at the robot teams looking as if they were ready for battle. The silence was deafening. What happened? Were they under attack?

Nicholas put his index finger to his lips begging for silence. He walked towards the door to the elevator and cocked his head to listen while he pointed his monitor to detect movement. The rustling noise was indeed coming from inside the elevator.

Then the door opened, and standing before the startled crowd were creatures or entities draped in brown robes. No faces, arms, legs or feet were visible, although the fabric moved ever so slowly as the visitors entered the hall and then stopped before Nicholas, his armies of robots and the Earthlings.

Ara dropped to the floor, and Jordan rushed to pick her up as she lay there moaning and rolling her eyes. Joan and Gladys grasped each other and attempted to hold each other up and remain still and quiet. Donald and Vicky looked at each other and tried not to laugh from a place inside them that was trembling and terrorized.

The remaining travelers remained in place as if they were stuck to the floor and could not move. Everyone was waiting for Nicholas or Jane to make the first move.   Jane walked towards the figures with her hands out in front of her as if she were going to embrace her mother. She made a soft humming voice with a melody sounding like *a Moonlight Sonata,*" and she continued to drift towards the figures who did not move or recoil. Instead one figure enveloped her in the folds of his garment and rocked slowly back and forth. Everyone watched with awe, but Nicholas appeared to be ready to order an attack while appearing to be calm and collected.

The other draped figures began to walk around and drape themselves over objects as if they were trying to feel the texture. They did not destroy tables, chairs or lamps. They seemed to be subsuming them or perhaps taking pictures of them; and as they moved around the hall, they avoided contact with the teams of robots standing on alert but set their sights on unfamiliar objects and the group of humans huddled in the back of the room.

Following Jane's lead, the Earthlings allowed themselves to be enveloped and examined all the while standing in complete silence and serenity as if they were receiving a benediction from some priestly figure. Even Ara who had revived, stood like a marble statue and breathed calmly.

Nicholas thought, "What is happening here? Are we being put under a spell? Jane seemed okay, but should I let this go on? What is going to happen next?"

The figure who appeared to be the leader moved from Jane to Nicholas, and slowly swathed him, held Nicholas tightly and moved slowly forward and back. It looked like Nicholas was being rocked to sleep. The cloaked figures released everyone and made their way back to the elevator cab, got in and magically disappeared up the shaft.

The group of residents, plus Nicholas and Jane, and it seemed even the robot assembly were in shock. It seemed like a lifetime of silence and shallow breathing until Joshua began to laugh.

"Well, I'll be damned," Joshua spoke and broke the spell. "That was a totally unexpected event. I thought I would be scared out of my mind when I first saw them, but then I felt a sudden release and peace. It was like a religious experience."

"Yes, I agree with you. It was as if I was having a mystical moment," Donald added as he moved to clasp his hands in prayer.

Vicky, the other Irish Catholic in the group, agreed with Donald. "It reminded me of my days at a traditional Catholic mass. I even thought I smelled incense. What an experience!"

"I had none of those feelings," Ernest said in his usual provocative voice. "I thought we should have shot them all and then ripped those shrouds of off them so we could see what was underneath."

The rest of the group showed their disagreement and contempt by huddling closer together and holding on to each other. Each of them expressed their unity by confirming Joshua's comments. There was no concern about religious affiliation, no haggling about different religious principles – they were united. Christians, Jews, Muslims and atheists experienced a spiritual awakening that brought them out of their petty worlds and into a sense of community and purpose.

Nicholas took command and responded to Ernest's outburst, "I don't see any reason for that kind of violence. They didn't threaten or attack, and they were peaceful and friendly. It may have been a ploy, but we will have to wait and see, especially since we are probably the interlopers on their planet."

"How do you know they didn't brain wash us

with all that hugging? They might have sent us mental messages to keep us passive," Ernest tries again to push forward his views on his neighbors.

"I think we have to trust Commander Nicholas' judgment on this and not become hostile and paranoid," Gladys offered, speaking in a calm and rational manner.

Nicholas felt supported and respected as he told his charges, "Let's sleep on this, and I will conduct further investigations on our visitors' origin and how they managed to commandeer the elevator. I will begin that process now by contacting our team on Earth and ask them if they had any knowledge about the inhabitants on Ymir. Perhaps they will be as surprised as we were; and if that is the case then we will work out a plan on how to proceed."

Ernest persisted and was joined in his skepticism by Charles who was beginning to have second thoughts. "Do you really trust your bosses on Earth? They certainly didn't give us all of the details regarding this mission? I would guess that they knew of our unlikely neighbors and wanted to see how we would react."

"Can we do anything to monitor the situation or must we put all our faith in you and your team of robots? Perhaps we could establish something like a neighborhood watch to see if these intruders visit us again – this time in a threatening way," Jordan questioned the commander.

"That might be a good idea, Jordan! Why don't you organize the group and make up a schedule for me and Jane? We will make sure you won't be disturbed, and a corps of robots will cover for you." Nicholas tried to sound reassuring but couldn't be sure if he was or not.

Jordan, hoping that he could use his Glock 19 that he had secretly kept in his space suit pocket, eagerly asked, "Will we be armed?"

Nicholas recoiled. It had never occurred to him that his charges would have brought firearms to Ymir. He had not thought to ask or conduct searches. He was a peaceful man and thought that any violence against the space travelers would be taken care of by the military arm of the robots.

"Does anyone have any weapons on their bodies or in their condo units?"

There was silence as the members looked around at each other. No one ventured forward, but Donald looked directly at Jordan and motioned to Nicholas.

Jordan had been identified and decided to answer the Commander's question.

"I do, Nicholas, I brought my Glock 19 with me and smuggled it in my space suit. I wanted to protect Ara and myself."

"Jordan, hand it over. We don't need to have anyone with a weapon here on Ymir. We have a defensive force to rely on in case of attack."

"Commander, I need to keep it with me. It is one of my prized possessions from my military service."

"Jordan, you will get it back when we return to Earth. Now hand it over to me – barrel down."

Chapter 9
All Hands on Deck

Waiting and watching, the earthlings gathered every night before dinner in order to discuss the current state of affairs. There were two camps and one outlier who did not fit into either mode. Joan, Kate, Joshua, Gladys, Vicky and Donald believed that a peace loving, gentle approach should be taken with Nicholas, Jane and the aliens.

Charles, Jordan and Ara were the hawks who wanted a more aggressive stance against the commander, his girl Friday and a warlike, tribal approach to the shrouded visitors. Ernest wanted out. He wanted to demand that Nicholas arrange for a quick retreat into the spacecraft so that they could all return home.

He spoke in no uncertain terms to his neighbors, "We were brought here under false circumstances, truth has been withheld, and now we find that we are not alone on this god-forsaken planet. We do have some rights, don't we?"

At that moment, Nicholas appeared in the doorway and strolled in with folders coddled under his arms. "I heard you, Ernest, but I have some good news and some bad news. I know that you are frightened and wondering about this planet, your command team and these ethereal visitors, and I want to re-assure you that you are safe. Having said that, I have been told to inform you about the conditions on planet Earth, our home."

"Inform us of what? What are you talking about?" Ernest yelled. His neighbors appeared to agree with his tone of voice and certainly identified with his anxiety when hearing the phrase, 'conditions on Earth.'

"There have been many catastrophes since we left our home planet. A few months ago, two hostile nations started a nuclear war with each other, and since they were distant neighbors, they unleashed powerful atomic weapons that spilled dangerous radiation throughout the atmosphere. That caused other nations to fire missiles with atomic warheads at their own neighbors whom they suspected of planning invasions.
Ten million people and animals were annihilated in the area between the two initial combatants, and another two million in the ensuing attacks. Following those horrors post-urban terror teams started transmitting atavistic horror videos of tribal warfare on every continent.

People started getting ill and dying from some mysterious disease. That, too, was broadcast and incited mobs of people trying to escape. The United Nations had made attempts at peaceful negotiations; however, skirmishes had still been occurring and the representatives were ignored and killed."

"Who were the original attackers and where did they originate?" Jordan asked since he had relatives in Texas and children in Arizona.

"Oh, my God," Gladys exclaimed, joining the others in shock and despair, "What can we do to contact our families?"

Nicholas did not answer but continued, "There are other problems that have arisen recently – torrential rains have caused major rivers to overflow their banks in Asia, Russia, Europe and North America, and if that weren't enough the warming temperatures have resulted in melting ice packs, raising sea levels and flooding cities throughout the world."

"This sounds like a Biblical Noah story. What are humans doing?" Donald asked as he tried to come to terms with his racing thoughts about his grandchildren who lived near the Ohio River.

"I can't tell you more than what I have reported. I have been trying to contact NASA, but the satellites are not operational at this time. Earth has descended into a digital wilderness."

"What does that mean for us, Nicholas?" How will we get our food? How will we return to Earth?" Ernest demanded.

"As far as the food is concerned, we have enough of the freeze-dried supplies to last us 2-3 months. We are stepping up our game in the development of our own food supply. The last report indicated that we are well on our way to becoming independent."

"I wanted to go back home," Ernest continued in his demanding way. "I have had enough of this mission, this environment and this life."

Nicholas answered in a quiet, patient voice, trying to keep his cool with this mad hatter of the group, "I am afraid that a return home is not possible at this time. We have minimal communication but have been told that all deliveries and transportation have been cancelled for the foreseeable future. That was the last message delivered from Earth."

"Will we ever get to go home?" Joan and Vicky responded in unison.

"Why would you want to go home? Planet Earth sounds as if it is in a death spiral." Joshua moaned and responded as he wiped his eyes and hung his head in dismay.

Jane, who had walked in during the exchanges, said, "Let's take this one day at a time. We can't go anywhere now, and we have some work to do to make this place more habitable and safe for us. This will have to be a team effort, folks. We all have some grieving to do, and we have to do it alone and together."

Nicholas walked towards Jane, embraced her, kissed her forehead and said, "This is the voice of reason and sanity."

Chapter 10
A Collection of Souls

Jordan called a meeting of the residents for the next morning at 10AM, saying "Let's all try to get some sleep or rest and meet to discuss this new information. Perhaps we could gather in our place."

The weary, worried earthlings nodded in agreement and slowly made their way back to their apartments. Having nothing to say to one another, they stayed in their heads trying to come to terms with this overwhelming news. The whole picture was unreal. This manufactured environment was a mirage. They began to think that this had been a bad dream, hoping that when they awoke, they would have returned to their real homes on beautiful blue Planet Earth with their real families and friends.

Most tried to sleep, but thoughts raced by like a train going across the horizon. Jumping from one thought to another, their brains seemed jumbled. Focus and concentration were impossible with all the half-completed thoughts wrapped in a taco of fear and anxiety. Feeling alone and abandoned, they could not enjoy the comfort of spouses or friends. Alone, they were, in their own heads and hearts, on this speck in the universe.

Upon awakening from his fitful sleep, Jordan scurried around to tidy up the apartment before folks arrived. He had not slept well, and Ara had been up and down all night long making it impossible for him to rest. He had tried to comfort her, but she was inconsolable. She kept mumbling to herself and then would pray to Allah to help her return to her grandparents' home in Iran. She surmised that Iran would not be flooded or hot with radiation. She had not kept herself informed about the country and its role in world affairs so that her fantasies were not in accordance with the reality. Muslims, she thought, would be saved from annihilation.

Jordan wondered about her mental health. What could he do? What would the neighbors say if they saw her like this? He wished he had a Valium or some kind of pill to calm her down.

"Ara, perhaps you should not attend the meeting."

"I am going to attend this meeting because I can't be by myself, and I want to know how others have been handling this. Don't patronize me. I'm quite capable of taking care of myself."

"Okay, okay. I was just trying to be helpful," Jordan responded with an irritated tone. He left the living room and went to get another cup of coffee.

When he returned, Ara had left and could be heard weeping in the bathroom. The bell rang, and he welcomed Donald and Vicky to come in and sit down. They both looked exhausted and morose.

"Well this is a fine mess, isn't it? By the way, where is Ara?" Donald inquired.

"She is powdering her nose and wiping her eyes. She has been very upset," Jordan tried to make light conversation.

"Well, I don't know anyone in this building who isn't," Vicky added. I don't think I slept more than one hour. I just kept tossing and turning. I even took my childhood teddy bear down from the shelf and cuddled with it all night."

They heard a knock on the door, and Jordan rose to welcome Joan and Ernest. They entered the room, went straight to the couch, sitting in stony silence.

Luckily, the remaining neighbors and Jane made their entrances and tried to make small talk to cut through the dark clouds.

"So, Jordan, what is the agenda today? Or do we just sit here, play 'ain't it awful' and cry together? I hope it isn't an EST meeting," Ernest assumed his usual provocative tone.

Jordan got out of his chair and moved to a marker board he had found in one of his closets and opened the meeting, "I call this meeting to order, and since we are probably being recorded and videoed, I see no reason to take minutes. We are not in an FBI vault where there is complete privacy."

"I love that idea. It will give us a framework to vent and to be creative and realistic about what we can do." Gladys enthusiastically gave Jordan support and the neighbors a sliver of hope.

"Let's begin by describing the situation we are in so we all start on the same page," Charles added using his lawyerly tone. "We are here on this planet deep in the cosmos, light years away from home. Our intrepid Commander, Nicholas Zervas, announced to us yesterday, Friday, May19, 2020 that Mother Earth had been stricken with floods, nuclear wars and unknown pathogens, killing more than the influenza virus did in 1918 and 1919 estimated to have been as high as 500 million people globally. All communication and transportation via Planet Express to Ymir had been cancelled for the foreseeable future. No payloads of food or equipment will be coming our way."

"Yes, and add that we have enough food for a few months," Vicky advised.

"Let's brainstorm and come up with any option, no matter how outrageous," Donald said since he had been a consultant to businesses and had run many brainstorming meetings.

"Who will be the recorder at the marker board? Someone who can write well and large so those of us with failing eyesight can easily read should be our scribe," Donald continued.

"Jane, would you be willing to help us?" Jordan asked.

"Surely, I will, but you did not notice that I was invited, but Nicholas was not." Jane wanted everyone to be clear about her position.

Donald responded in a matter of fact way, "Nicholas is our commander and would probably cramp our style, especially if we plan a mutiny."

The crowd snickered and looked to see how Jane reacted. They were not surprised to watch her face remain impassive and her body erect and motionless as was her habit. She remained as un-revealing as ever when she was not around Nicholas. She gestured that she was ready to begin.

"I say that we should confirm the information Nicholas told us regarding the status of planet Earth. Did he receive false news, doctored news in order to get us to stay here and not try to get back to our home," Ernest, the doubting Thomas said.

"If indeed we can't return for the foreseeable future, then how can we find out when the green-houses will be ready to help us feed ourselves," Joan seemed to have accepted the inevitable and focused on food. She was not ready to die by star-vation.

"How long will our robot friends be able to operate without communication from Planet Earth? Would their dysfunction cause them to quit working or rebel against us? I have grown ra-ther fond of them," Joshua added with a smile.

"Can we get an alternative form of communi-cation to contact Earth? I wonder if there isn't an-other planet we could visit, one with a conducive atmosphere," Charles said hopefully.

"Do we need to take some conservation measures to save our electricity – fewer travels to downtown or to the gym? I would not want to run out of electricity because we have been wasteful," Vicky wondered out loud.

"Do we have some pills to put us out of our misery in case everything implodes? We have to ask the Robotic doctors about that, I would imagine," Donald said, remembering that he had wished he had some Nembutal when his late wife lay suffering in great pain and called for him to help her.

Everyone remained silent for a few moments in order to entertain the possibility of disability and death, thoughts that usually did not enter their minds at any given moment.

Finally, Jane, who had been taking notes on her tablet, addressed the group and asked, "Does anyone else have any other ideas to add to this very pertinent list?"

Gladys stood up and said, "I think we should try to contact the figures who had visited us and who live on Ymir. They might have technologies we have not developed."

The neighbors gasped, but once they started breathing again, they thought the possibility was there. Why not?

"Jane, please note that in the minutes. We want that suggestion to make the rounds in the executive suite," Jordan instructed.

Chapter 11
A Motley Crew

Nicholas invited the Earthlings to his central command module and demonstrated the failure of all computers directly connected to Earth. He then pointed to his own specialized listening device that had connected him to satellite stations and NASA and to the teams of robots who stood at low frequency throughout the community.

"I figured that I have about 48 hours of connectivity if we keep everything operating at the utmost efficiency," Nicholas warned.

"We then have a short window of time to contact our hooded neighbors on surface Ymir to ask for help. Nicholas, we met and decided to attempt to get in contact with them," Gladys spoke, speaking for the group.

"Jane told me about your meeting and your ideas. You realize, don't you, that I could not monitor your gathering because of the energy situation. I assumed that you wanted me to do something about this so Jane and I rode to the surface and waited for their visit. The hooded ones appeared a few hours later, and much to our surprise they seemed to know of our plight, probably because of the reduced light emissions."

"Or perhaps they monitor us, and they have some sort of Googling Translate to tell them what we have been saying. It really doesn't matter how they found out. What can they do to help us? I am hoping for a miracle," Ernest turned his eyes toward Nicholas and spoke in a gentle, subdued tone.

"They do have an advanced translation system for inhabitants of many planets. They did not tell me where or how they live, but they wrote on a special device – I called it a Ymir pad– that translated simultaneously. They want to help us because so far, we have been peaceful and respectful of them. The first thing they will do is to deliver some solar panels so we can restore the normal energy needs of our compound."

"What do they want from us in return?" Charles asked.

"They have not requested anything so far except a request that we let them do this first step in complete secrecy and privacy. They do not want our help or peering eyes," Nicholas responded looking for re-assurance and support.

"They could use the solar panels to create so much heat that we all expire," paranoid Ara added.

"Ara, why would they do that? All they would have to do is wait and then swoop in and pick up the pieces, so to speak," Jordan answered as he tried to help her take a more optimistic view.

"Yes, we don't have many options open to us. We have to trust. When will they begin to construct the solar devices, and hook us up – or whatever they call the connection procedure," Gladys responded with enthusiasm.

"I believe they are up there already at work." Nicholas admitted to having made decisions before meeting with the neighbors."

Gladys laughed heartily and said, "I should have known that you would be one step ahead of us."

The lights were dim, the robots in rest mode, and the mood of the human family was blue with a rim of orange. The Earthlings had submitted to the present. They had managed to shred almost every piece of hope for eventual return to Mother Earth, and now they would make do and live their remaining days trying to stay alive and sane.

The enormity of their plight had produced a more peaceful tribe of inhabitants. The group seemed to have coalesced around survival, and those who had been more critical, competitive and annoying had moved towards a gentler, co-operative state. The older ones thought they were in the foxhole, that they should act like good soldiers and support one another.

Ernest had become kinder and gentler towards the women and sparred less often with the men or with Nicholas. He had been writing a memoir and examining his life. This had led to a realization that he had been a selfish, stubborn and sanctimonious snob who had alienated three wives, two children, friends and family. He had lived alone for the past five years because he could find no woman who could tolerate him, and now he had turned his neighbors against him. His insights had encouraged him to change his behavior and his thinking about the value of other human beings, and now he was determined to feel kindly towards the nonhumans who co-habited this planet – his new home. Perhaps, he thought, he could find redemption in this new life.

Joan had noticed the new Ernest but had chosen to be wary since she had observed his 'change on a dime' personality. She certainly could use his help when she couldn't reach to change a light bulb, but she tried to be as independent as she could at her age. Turning eighty had been a shock to her especially since arthritis and high blood pressure attended her birthday party and then refused to leave.

Joan had not relied on her neighbors – not on Earth or here on Ymir – but she began to think that given the circumstances, her snobby attitude towards them should be tempered. There was to be no more 'kiss up and kick down.' They were all fine people with a few quirks, but who was she to talk. She was not a long-term relationship queen. Her late husband had been patient and placating since he felt lucky to have a lovely woman who could love a short, unattractive man.

She and Charles Trainor shared these personality traits and had been regarded as snobby, yet treacherous in their ability to attack people verbally to show them how superior they were. Charles had become less lawyerly and had been in touch with a grandfatherly part of his personality.

He had been irritable and demeaning to his wife, Kate, when he was in pain from gout or bad knees; but since the discovery of the horrors on planet Earth, he had been grieving with her, fearing for his children and grandchildren with whom he could now have no contact. He, too was coming around to becoming a team player.

The remainder of the group had realized the nature of their predicament, surrendered to the idea that they had few choices and wanted to make the best of a frightening situation. They were all experiencing some anticipatory grieving the probable loss of their loved ones and of their original home.

One evening, they gathered together and formed a grief group where they could express their sorrows while remembering. Some had managed to sneak a few pictures of grandchildren into their clothing before donning their space suits; and as they took them out of their hiding places, they cried and gave eulogies about the sweetness of grandchildren. At the end of the two-hour session, they decided to meet again the following week and continue the process.

At this moment, however, they had more important work to do in order to guarantee their survival. Now that light and heat would be restored, they decided to concentrate on the next big subsistence project – growing their own food – and enlisting the shrouded people to help them. Once the energy requirements were restored, they could help Nicholas find the programs for seed and soil selection that had been developed by NASA and installed by the farmer robot teams.

"Let's ask Nicholas where the team is in terms of greenhouse horticulture," Gladys spoke and offered to contact him with her question.

"Why don't we ask him to attend one of our meetings so we can all get to hear what he has to say. He can't be too busy to inform us," Joshua asked as he contemplated the fact that he would not be acting or producing documentaries on his adventure in space anytime soon.

Gladys and the others nodded in agreement. She would locate him and ask him to attend one or all of our daily meetings to give us the latest news briefing and answer our next pressing question.

The group had coalesced, and in spite of the fact that they were strange bedfellows, they began to avoid bickering and work as a team.

Chapter 12
This is No Gourmet Feast

The meeting began with Nicholas describing the progress of the horticulture project. They could begin to grow their own greenhouse vegetables and fruit within two months now that heat and light sources were available. Having meat products available was quite another matter. The cloning research was ongoing but was slow in producing viable embryos of sheep or cows.

"Of course, we will have to rely on the beans we are growing for our protein," Nicholas said as he attempted to moderate their hopes.

"Those shrouded figures must eat something, don't you think? Perhaps they have built some kind of greenhouse to grow some of their food. Why don't we contact them and see if we couldn't build some kind of partnership?" Gladys asked in a pleading voice.

"Let's wait until they finish with the solar panels, and then a few of us can ride up and wait for them to visit us again," Nicholas responded with a hopeful tone, happy to see that his charges had come around to a spirit of cooperation and willingness to accept things they could not change. Now they seemed to be willing to explore what they could change.

"We had better not wait too long because our food will run out, and we won't be getting any deliveries," Donald reminded everyone of the need for action.

"All of this talk about food is making me hungry for a good steak. Do we have any left?" Joshua inquired, "But I think we had better begin to ration the freeze-dried victuals just in case things take longer than expected."

Jane added in her usual official-Jane tone, "We had begun the process the day before yesterday. We were treating it like a withdrawal from alcohol but without the symptoms. Slow and steady reduction in the portion sizes and the animal protein. Now we have to figure out what the replacements will be in order to keep you guys from getting urges."

"I think Jane and Nicholas should be the leaders in contacting and negotiating with the Shrouded Ones," Joan added.

"Well, thanks, Joan, for your vote of confidence, but we need two of you to accompany us – those with cool heads and nonthreatening attitudes. I suggest that you decide on the representatives and make a list of questions you would like them to answer," Nicholas answered with firmness as he did not want to be the only one responsible for mission failure.

"I vote for Charles and Kate since they are the perfect couple to do this. She will offset his lawyerly approach with tact and openness. She also takes good notes and knows how to listen," Gladys offered her quick and accurate assessment.

"When do we start?" Charles immediately took up the challenge and offered himself and his wife. Kate nodded in agreement.

"I will go up tonight and check on their progress with the current energy project and make some gestures to let them know how grateful we are."

"Nicholas, take them a gift – an apple. Then watch and see what they do with it when they see you putting one in your mouth and chewing it. That way you might discover whether there is a face and mouth under the drapery," Ernest said with some pride in his inventiveness.

"Two apples from our dwindling stock? Yes, I think that is a good idea. It might work. Food has been a bridge between different people on our planet," Nicholas responded and rose to leave the meeting.

"Do you think you will need protection?" Jordan offered.

"We are in no position to use force to fight or even defend ourselves, Jordan," Ara responded with a warning look at her partner. "You are not in the military anymore."

"How about bringing a new outfit for one of them. They could use a little color," Gladys added with a wry humor which immediately led to outbursts of laughter and silly suggestions for gifts , such as shoes, gloves or sunglasses, that Nicholas could take with him on his mission.

Chapter 13
The Art of the Deal on Ymir

Nicholas, Jane, Charles and Kate donned space gear, said their good byes and got into the elevator. Jane pushed the button and the old Otis-like machine quickly moved upward. Energy levels had been totally restored, and the group quickly made their way to the surface. Opening the door, they walked out and stood at a reasonable distance from the elevator.

They spoke in whispers although there was no one in sight. The wait gave them time to examine the landscape. It was a desolate place with ice and snow-covered mounds, hills and holes or crevices. They wanted to explore but were afraid to walk or take off their breathing helmets and suits for fear that they would get lost in this glacial desert.

Perhaps the hooded ones were exhausted from their work on the solar panels and would not appear. Did they need their rest as humans do or do they just keep going as do the robots? There were so many unknowns. There were so many questions the humans wanted to ask, but they knew that establishing a relationship would not be easy. They must be patient and respectful until they could be given one of the translation pads which would allow them to dialogue.

Nothing was changing in the environment, and the wait seemed eternal until a soft rustling sound alerted the humans to approaching figures in the distance. As they neared, one stepped forward with its tablet-like pad and showed it to Nicholas who read the message to his team members.

'Do you have other needs?'

Nicholas wrote in English on the pad that was made available but not handed over to him, "We would like to share our knowledge of nutrients with you and learn about your nutritional needs."

'Our diet is sparse, and we would like to know how you get your food and what it is like.'

"I think that we could work together to help each other. Our planet, Earth, is not able to communicate with us or deliver supplies to us. We have been growing plants in our greenhouses," Nicholas offered cooperation so that they would not think we would be doing them a favor by being the dominant group. "Would it be possible for a group of you to join us in our bunker to learn of our ways?"

'We will consult with our people and let you know about a collaboration. As far as we know we are the only communities on this planet. We were banished from our galaxy and our home when asteroids destroyed our homes and marauding groups of aliens arrived to take over the planet. A group of survivors managed to commandeer a space craft that had been designed to come to this planet.'

"So we have many things in common. We wish that there was a better way to communicate with you. We do not have any similar devices that translate from your language to ours," Jane stepped forward and wrote on the pad as Nicholas stepped aside.

'Perhaps that problem could be solved.'

"That certainly would make it easier to work together for our mutual benefit," Kate wrote and continued to smile and reach out to these strange but peaceful creatures.

All parties made gestures of imminent departure: nods, hand waves, blowing of kisses and rustling of fabrics. The earthlings had struggled to make movements that would look peaceful given the weight of their space suits while the shrouded ones revealed nothing of their body type. The mystery remained, but the humans were satisfied with what had been achieved and made their way back to the elevator to report the promising news.

Nicholas called for a meeting of the group as soon as they arrived at the compound while Charles and Kate struggled to remove their space gear.

Charles then came forward as spokesperson, "We have some good news to report to you. We discovered more information about our neighbors who showed interest in cooperating with us to develop our agriculture program. They also showed positive responses to Jane's request for more assistance in communication between us.

We will await their final decision once they have discussed the issues with their community.”

“What a hopeful report. Thank you. It sounds as if these shrouded ones are more civilized and democratic than humans,” Gladys responded with her usual upbeat voice.

“They, too, were sent to another planet when an asteroid brought destruction and havoc to their planet. Marauding tribes brought more chaos, and they were sent to Ymir.” Kate added.

“These immigrants must have learned something from their experience,” Jane said. “Let’s hope we can do the same.”

Chapter 14
Diversity on Ymir

Thirty hooded ones took turns going down the elevator to the human community. They were wearing special square box-like structures over the top part of their shrouds since they realized from written conversations with Nicholas that they could not breathe the oxygen that was pumped into the bunker through a pipeline that led to a central grid and condenser that converted electricity to oxygen.

The human group met and welcomed them with gestures. They carried a container that held the translation pads and proceeded to open it and hand one to each of the humans.

"Thank you, thank you, "Jane wrote on her pad while she proceeded to show the others the ease of operating these tablet-like devices they had brought from Earth.. It was as if she had seen them before and had been familiar with the gadgets and with the shrouded figures who had gifted the tools to the humans.

Nicholas stood by her and began to write the plan for their visit. Each member of the human tribe stood by one of the shrouded figures as they began to walk towards the greenhouses. They communicated to one another using their translation pads and appeared to speak on friendly terms, and the humans were careful to avoid asking questions about their garb or their bodies.

Upon entering the greenhouse, Nicholas began to write about the different plants and the technology of hydroponic or soil-based agriculture and their hopes of becoming self-sustaining in the near future and reminding them that without their help with the solar panels all would be lost.

'*We are impressed* with *your technology since we subsist on a diet of algae that grows in some of the crevices we have explored. We also melt the ice on the surface for drinking. Our shrouds hide our body form and protect us from the extreme cold of living near the surface of the planet, even though we can withstand extremely cold temperatures.*'

"Would we be able to help you by having you work in our greenhouses and share our harvest?" Ernest wrote on his pad and handed it to Nicholas.

Nicholas had already seen the question and looked to the hooded ones to respond. "We certainly would like to share what we know and learn what you know. In that way, we could make a better existence for all of us."

'*I think we could accomplish this if we could work peacefully and cooperatively.*'

Then the shrouded figures loosened their garments and stood in front of their new neighbors who watched in sheer astonishment. The figures who stood before them were tall bipedal creatures with brown skin, showing eight digits ending in a grip on long arms and feet that were wide and curved at the end. Their heads were encased in the breathing apparatus – not visible.

'Now that you see us for who we are, are you still willing to have us as partners?'

"I see no reason we can't all live together in peace and harmony as we are all trying to survive on this dreary planet," Jane wrote and was joined by the other humans who knew that this venture could benefit all and let them endure.

"We will develop a plan and send it to you so you can make suggestions or revamp it."

'We are hoping that most of us can work with you on site. The remaining team would remain in our compound to keep things running and alert us if other beings want to take what we have.'

The Brown figures picked up their shrouds and headed for the elevator while the humans stood frozen in space wondering what had just happened. No one expected to see what they had just witnessed. They had all been acquainted with humans of a different skin color on earth, and each one considered themselves to be post-racist.

This was a different situation – these creatures were of a different color in addition to being a varied body form. They wondered what their heads would look like. Did they have eyes, mouths, nostrils, a brain? Would they ever find out? Did it really matter? They were all too old to think of procreation. Marriage, cohabitation and DNA exchange were all possibilities for their cloned selves in the future should that happen.

Returning to the group of anxious humans, Nicholas waited to hear their reactions.

"I have racing thoughts about these creatures, Nicholas. There are so many questions I have about them and their intentions. Could they be wanting to work with us now to learn about our technology in order to exploit us before they do away with us?" Ernest said as his cynical, suspicious-self returned.

"Come on, Ernest," Gladys responded, "Do we have a choice? They could put us in the dark in a moment. Furthermore, we are old enough to have few expectations of a long life here on Ymir or on Planet Earth."

"We have to go on faith. There is no rational approach to determine their motives," Kate responded.

"Amen to that," the humans replied in prayer-like unison.

Chapter 15
Life as We Know It Is Gone

As the teams of humans and Ymirians toiled in the greenhouses, they continued to communicate with the Ymir pads, and in some cases, they would touch hands or digits of the other and let out a squeal of delight. The humans would smile and make a whistling sound while their brown-skinned companions came through with a loud exhale.

At the end of their work time the visitors would wrap their cloaks tightly and make their way to their home while the humans would return to their building, collapse into their chairs and nap. Nicholas and Jane, however, returned to the greenhouses to assess the work that had been done that day.

"It is amazing that we have been able to hasten the process of growing our plants and hopefully increasing our harvest. This team of humans, robots and creatures from Ymir have done wonders and have been cooperative and peaceful," Nicholas boasted.

"True, but, sweetheart, I take issue with you calling the Ymirians creatures. They are no more creatures than we are. There are no distinctions, just different physical attributes. We are all different forms of alternate universes, but overall, we are part of the same creation or Creator," Jane lectured her partner who rolled his eyes but gave her a pat on the head and a kiss on her lips. Their relationship had blossomed.

"What do you suggest we call them, dearest one?" Nicholas asked with a smirk and a smile.
"How about partners for now? As we learn more we can plan a formal baptism and include them in the ritual. They would probably like that," Jane offered to help Nicholas in his quest for empathy and kindness.

"Okay, I get it. I was also wondering whether we might be able to get some of their DNA if they have such material in their cells and combine it with cells from us to see if we could engineer a mutation that would allow them to breathe oxygen. If that could happen we would discover what kind of head, face and brain they have. Wouldn't that be cool?" Nicholas asked in his usual ten-steps-ahead fantasies.

"One step at a time, Nicholas. Let's just figure out how we are going to feed ourselves and allow them to take their share of the harvest home and determine the best way for them to feed themselves," Jane responded in her own matter-of-fact way.

As they headed back to the main house, they heard the elevator making a descending sound. The door opened, and a group of Browns appeared. They took out their pads and wrote,

'When we went back home, we encountered a

group of gray-hooded creatures who stood by our crater that we call home. They carried no weapons but seemed anxious to communicate. They did not have any means of communications so we rustled up a few of our pads and wrote a message. They have a language and responded that they had been displaced from their homes on this planet by groups of marauding creatures with whitish skin, heads covered with globe-like helmets and long pointed rods ready to pierce any other being. They wanted to come and live with us.'

"What a surprise that must have been for you. Do you have a choice? You do not appear to us humans as warring parties, but it also sounds like these warrior tribes might be approaching your and our homes and have war in mind. If you choose to let the gray-hooded ones share your community, you should let us know. Then we three communities can meet to discuss what we must do to defend ourselves from these invader types," Nicholas spoke with an air of knowing experience with violent beings.

'We agree that we do not have much choice, and furthermore, we may need more beings to defend ourselves from these invaders. You have a few fighters and some robots, and we have about one hundred of us. We can utilize more defenders whatever color they happen to be. Let's keep our farming project among ourselves until we know more about our guests.'

"We have a plan, and I will inform my group. Let's meet tomorrow night to discuss our plans for security," Nicholas suggested, knowing full well that his group would be ready to develop a system of resistance since all of them had been informed of security measures on Earth when terrorists tried to destroy their civilization. Television, movies and their government had taught them about reacting to violence."

Nicholas was certain that his Earthlings would respond appropriately to help him and Jane prepare for their defense, and his conclusions were affirmed when he met his people.

"Of course, we have to get our robots armed with spears, knives, bows and arrows, and guns. Most of us have no experience defending ourselves or using weapons," Ernest hastened to offer his approval.

"We don't have any of those items unless someone has sneaked guns to Ymir or Nicholas has a hidden cache. Is there any way we could try diplomacy with these white-skin invaders? We do have something in common," Vicky offered, hoping that they would not have to repeat the mistakes made on Earth.

"When those violent tribal beings show their intent by banishing people, they continue to expand their spheres of influence and take over territory," Jordan, the former military man, stated.

Nicholas interceded, "I think Jordan has a point. If they have been violent against others before, they are more likely to do it again. We don't know, and we have no way of finding out the real truth. Let's arm ourselves just in case."

"It's better to be safe than sorry," Jane concurred, "and the only weapon we could possibly use is to make sure they could not enter our world through the elevator and help our neighbors find some way of keeping them from entering their home from the surface. We don't have guns nor ways to make steel rods."

"Deception and camouflage are our best bet for the present time while we explore weapons for the future," Jordan argued.

"It's déjà vu," Vicky reiterated in a despairing tone, "This is the beginning of the end of this world, too."

Chapter 16
The Immigration Crisis Resolution

Was this going to be the war to end all wars on Ymir? The Grays moved in with the Browns until they were chased out by the marauders. Leaving everything behind, they all approached the community of the crevice and moved in with the Earthlings who made peace with each other and their visitors.

What choice would they have had since their small community was defenseless and isolated. As they descended into the crevice, they found spaces to accommodate their tribes. The village was enlarged to accommodate the immigrants; and in time, the Grays, Browns and Humans worked together to design and manufacture hidden upright warrior robots which they stationed outside the elevator door on the surface thereby placing a defensive net around their entry.

It turned out that the Grays possessed prodigious design capabilities that complemented the engineering strengths of the Browns. While the Humans on Ymir had to forsake the technological assistance of Earth-bound NASA, they had become expert in organization, maintenance communication and biological research. They had accumulated supplies of metals and substances from Ymir's surface and combined these resources with those brought from Earth to assemble devices and develop food for their subsistence.

The inhabitants began to feel safer together as a diverse yet stable society. Occasionally they could hear loud noises from metals clashing – then silence. This went on for years in Earth time yet there was no piercing of the perimeter security.

Horticulture flourished as did the creativity of the different beings who cooperated and coordinated their efforts to stabilize and improve their community. Skirmishes did arise among individuals but were quickly resolved by the council of elders who realized that they were not living in a post-racist society yet. The aging Earthling community, having heard that they could return to Earth if they could withstand a long trip on a re-conditioned space ship, made the decision to stay put. If new information became available concerning the conditions at home, then they would re-consider.

The group of Humans began to give into their mortal bodies leaving the younger Nicholas and Jane to represent their tribe and procreate more of themselves. As the minority, they chose to stay on peaceful Ymir, crevice 101, and make the best of it. There was so much to do and so much to learn that Earth appeared as a dream that they had forgotten. As a self-sustaining underground world, the Ymirians as they now all called themselves decided to dedicate themselves to building and maintaining their world for as long as they could while knowing that death and destruction could someday come to their world plunging them into an ever-changing galaxy.

seeking . . .

part two

Chapter 17
The New Adventure

The creatures of brown, gray and white skin or shrouds had adjusted to their crevice life during the two-and-one-half earth-time years since their arrival and were trying to make the best of their limited existence. Defenses had been erected and marauders beaten back. The greenhouses were producing food to sustain the community, and the diverse inhabitants had brought their own special food items, grafted onto the available grain plants, resulting in edible foodstuffs for everyone. The Browns and Grays had adapted to the expansion of their vegetarian algal regimen. For Humans, the diet was lacking in their favorite proteins, beef and eggs, but they agreed that the vegetarian substitutes suited the needs of all of their neighbors.

The cloning project was still in process of discovery. There were many complaints from the Earth residents that they missed eating meat, and they hoped that a suitable alternative would be developed before their return to Mother Earth where they could enjoy a hamburger or hotdog. A soybean, or what they thought was soybean, hamburger was not a good substitute; but they did not give up hope that the Robot science team would come up with a better recipe. Every day was a new challenge, but the inhabitants worked together to forge an inclusive community of others.

Commander Nicholas had kept peace and order, but he was getting bored with the status quo. He and Jane had finally made a commitment to each other and were planning to start a family to replenish the human stock. However, Nicholas pined for a new challenge, a project that would inspire him as the trip to Ymir with the small gang of seniors had done for him.

He had encouraged a group of unlikely travelers to bond, expand their horizons, and to accept creatures other than Earthlings. He had created a peaceful community and a defensive perimeter. His work as leader was diminished, and he missed the thrill of discovery and the challenge of war-like defenses. Perhaps it was that the Homo sapiens gene for survival demanding resolve and a blind eye for violence had weakened in this atmosphere. Only the threat of extinction motivated him on Ymir.

Jane had been a perceptive and willing partner for Nicholas. She supported his policies when it pertained to Ymir and Ymirians, and softened his toughness with reason and affection, but now she saw that the fire had gone out of his eyes and his heart.

"Nicholas, you need to take a trip."

"What? A trip to where?" Nicholas stepped back in surprise.

Jane reached for his hand and stroked his palm, "I see in my dreams that you are destined to return to Planet Earth and bring us news. Should we begin to plan a return to our original home?"

"And how would I get there, my dear dreamer? Walk? Fly? By free will?" Nicholas answered with a smile and an affectionate nudge.

"Our original space vehicle is still up on the surface of Ymir. We have a fighting force to keep away the marauders, and the technical skills of the Browns to repair and restore the ship to its original working shape and to create a Saturn-type rocket to blast you off into space," Jane pressed on with reason and logic,

"This could be a challenge for all of us technologically while psychologically the results of your findings would either continue to give us hope for a return home or put our fears and anxiety to rest and ultimately be able to move on with our reality."

"I thought we were going to start our family. We have to do what we can to keep our species alive since our fellow humans are too old to reproduce."

Jane smiled and responded with a wink and a firmer pressure on Nicholas' palm, "We can start that process right now, and the prospect of a little bundle of joy will make you a very cautious traveler and one who won't tarry on his mission."

Nicholas' eyes burned as they had in the past as he rose to embrace his Jane, his partner and his muse, "Let's get started."

"On both projects?" Jane laughed and snuggled in Nicholas's arms.

Chapter 18
Preparations

Jane was right – the Browns possessed the superior technical skills needed to repair the spacecraft – working in the dead of night for fear that their neighbors below would become anxious if they knew that their beloved leader would be leaving them. It was better to wait until the departure time was closer when he would make a speech and entrust them with the care of their community and, more importantly, the care of his hopefully pregnant partner and fellow conspirator, the precious Jane.

Scouring the surface of Ymir and utilizing the research laboratory NASA had established to construct the buildings, vehicles and infrastructure of the crevice community, the Browns and the Engineer bots toiled to bring the spacecraft lying quietly where it had landed back to its functional life. The space shuttle had been damaged during landing and required hours of painstaking engineering to return it to its former appearance and to repair the antennas, control sensors and landing gear. Its delicately constructed skin was covered with special silica tiles, insulated so that the underlying structure would not be damaged.

The next step and the most dangerous was to construct and to load the space shuttle external cylinders containing the liquid hydrogen fuel and oxygen oxidizer. These would be transferred to the shuttle main engines in the orbiter, the winged vehicle, during lift off.

Once that was accomplished they set their sights on the development of booster rockets to launch the craft. For this, they enlisted the Grays who had skills in rocketry and explosives and who had experience mixing the fuel and the oxidizer to form a propellant that, when ignited, would combust and launch. The oxygen would have to be pumped from the laboratory in the community, and it would take two booster rockets with millions of pounds of fuel at a speed of at least 25,000 miles per hour to insure lift off and reach an orbital height where Commander Nicholas could take control of the orbiter. There was no Wernher von Braun to develop the perfect rockets, but the Grays had found records from NASA that described Saturn V. These rocket boosters would hopefully fall back to Ymir if and when their parachutes deployed.

Space for the astronaut had always been an issue for manned space travel. The robot engineering team had developed a modular-constructed rover that could be assembled from smaller parts. One traveler could reconstruct the vehicle while traveling through space, lower it onto the surface of a planet and direct the vehicle from inside. It could travel miles on the foam core wheels using radioisotope batteries as a power source. The one-man crew would live in its pressurized cabin for exploratory rides and return to the orbiter for food, rest and renewal of the low pressure oxygen in his spacesuit. Hopefully, the oxygen on Planet Earth would be safe to transfer to the traveler. No one had current knowledge about the various levels of atmosphere surrounding Planet Earth following years of warfare and climate changes.

Once the spacecraft was ready, Nicholas decided to call a meeting of his diverse community and tell him of the journey he had planned. He was uneasy about this communication, but he knew that they would understand and be supportive of his efforts to bring back information and any DNA from remaining plants and animals that could sustain and enrich their diets.

The Earthlings had become a cooperative and enthusiastic group. He remembered what a fractured bunch they had been when first brought to Ymir. But with the terrifying news of Earth's destructive events, they took a while to grieve and soon came to the realization that they were survivors. However, they were survivors believing in a return to Planet Earth.

Nicholas was well aware of the capacity for humans to deploy defensive mechanisms to relieve fears and anxiety, and the Earthlings had perfected denial and minimization to cope with their emotions. Nicholas would not interfere with or negate their psychological strategies.

Once the group gathered and settled into quiet

conversations with voice or translation devices, Jane called the meeting to order and introduced Nicholas who had donned his space suit minus the helmet for the occasion. Nicholas stood before his neighbors and began to speak.

"Hello, my dear friends...."

Before he had a chance to finish his sentence, the room burst into applause and laughter.

"You thought you could keep a secret from us," Gladys shouted, "but we have our ways to know about present and future events."

Both Jane and Nicholas were dumbfounded and asked, "How did you know and how long have you known?"

"Our eyes are still good, and we can hear in spite of our age, "Donald responded," plus some of us don't sleep well at night so we snoop around and check out the place. There is no longer any Ovaltine or Ambien here to insure peaceful slumber."

Gladys added, "We also have friends in high places who have extraordinary powers to do very important work but know that their loyalty to you does not diminish when news is shared with neighbors."

"Well, I'll be damned. This is indeed a surprise and a welcome relief to be sure. I was very nervous about sharing this news."

"And now," the painfully shy Ara said, "What other little tidbit of news do you have to tell us?"

All eyes shifted to Jane who sat by Nicholas and nibbled one cookie after another.

"You know about that, too?" Nicholas and Jane

were stunned that their little secret had been discovered. Perhaps the camera that had been installed in the apartment building could see more
than anyone thought.

Chapter 19
A Trip to the Past

The day of liftoff was uneventful because the Ymirians had planned the event ever so carefully. Quietly they hoisted the oxygen tanks up to the surface in the elevator and transferred the gas to the external tank to mix with the hydrogen. Robots and the engineering Browns in the control center checked all systems and declared that all was ready to blast off.

Nicholas had donned his space suit and helmet following an emotional goodbye to Jane who, despite her faith in the mission, secretly harbored fears and trepidations.

"What if the gases exploded? What if the trip through space took too long and Nicholas ran out of food and oxygen?" What ifs filled her active brain and unsettled her sleep and appetite that were already disturbed by morning sickness and hormonal disruptions. She had been accustomed to being a rational, logical and unemotional woman, and these physiological and psychological changes made it difficult to hold back the tears when she said goodbye to Nicholas and when she turned to her neighbors for support – a behavior that had previously never entered her consciousness.

The Humans and the shrouded Browns and Grays shared her distress. In one form or another, they experienced apprehension and fear. Humans cried, perspired profusely and held each other and Jane while the Browns shuddered under their robes and the Grays beamed lights on and off from their raised arms and clawed fingers. They all stood as one in a group deep in their crevice atmosphere while Nicholas was hoisted into the orbiter. A few moments later, the sky lit up as the space ship launched when the rockets fired and the tanks fell away. There was a moment of color orange and then silence and space.

Nicholas had been surprised by the speed of the vessel and the noise and shaking as it hurtled through the darkness of interstellar galactic space. His previous experience from Earth had not been so sudden and swift, and he wondered what the Grays had used or added to blast him off into space. Perhaps they had an Elon Musk character living among them. He checked the coordinates, communicated back to Ymir that he was on his way, and then he felt an enormous desire to sleep. He sat back into the space chair, closed his eyes and hoped that he would awaken refreshed and ready to work.

Time travel had been in the infancy stage on Planet Earth, but when Nicholas awoke from his slumber, he observed a familiar galaxy and realized that he was close to Planet Earth as he watched the spectacular rings of Saturn sweep by followed by red-spotted Jupiter, reddish Mars, golden-bright Venus and dark and tiny Mercury. How could he have missed massive Neptune and spinning Uranus with their distinctive colors and size? Swirling around the space craft in the Milky Way galaxy were asteroid fragments, smaller bodies resembling planets, and space junk floating around and being whipped away from the space craft itself.

And then, there it was – Planet Earth – that bluish object covered with whitish cloud cover. He recalled the original Earthrise picture taken by astronaut William Anders during Apollo 8's historic mission. At closer look, Nicholas noticed that what he thought was white was actually gray, giving Earth a dirty and fragile look, circling the sun but seeming somewhat off kilter. As the orbiter left the moon's gravitational pull, the spacecraft fell into the Earth's orbit. As Nicholas rotated around the planet, he photographed the ground as if he was mapping the surface. The camera lenses enabled cutting through the clouds and enlarging the images to see the terrain without making a landing.

He could hardly believe what he was seeing – massive destruction of cities with flattened buildings lying in rubble, twisted metal of what had been vehicles or bridges. Rivers were filled with ash and dust as dirty water carried corpses – or what he thought the specks of brown tarnished objects were – tree limbs and black rocks to the gray oceans. Forest areas were charred and covered with the ashes of the world that had been, and the fields in the mid-west had been burned away. Deserts were covered with gray sand breaking into mounds and valleys. Volcanos dotted the landscape with fire and lava that added to the dust and swirling cinders of the atmosphere. This was a stark contrast to what he remembered as a young man watching the pictures supplied by the astronauts in 1968.

When the spacecraft passed through the gray clouds, the rain that fell cascaded to earth in sheets while the snow brought the dark flakes swirling in the vicious winds. Mile after mile of complete destruction greeted Nicholas who desperately looked for any sign of life. He found only silence and emptiness. Sixteen orbits around the planet at various levels convinced him that landing on Planet Earth, his former home, would be dangerous and devastating for him.

"One more lap around, and then I will return home," he moaned as he readied the booster rockets that would lift him out of earth's orbit and into space.

As he looked back, he was surprised to see a lighter spot from Planet Earth, near the southern tip of North America that could possibly be Florida, but it was too late to turn back to explore what it might be. It seemed that even the familiar continents had moved or blurred, fracturing the landscape.

Chapter 20
The Return

Following his warm reception by the Browns who'd guided his landing with the help of computers and robots, Nicholas hurried to find Jane who was surprised and thrilled to see the father of her little girl, Leia, who had recently celebrated her second birthday. Seeing her, Nicholas was wonderstruck at this beautiful, fair-haired creature who had appeared during his absence. He had wondered how long his exploratory trip had taken. Would it have been three years?

He still thought in Earth time but realized that time on Ymir and in space was in another dimension. How could he have missed such an important event in his and Jane's life? Somehow he thought a trip back to Earth would be like going across the pond or to the grocery store. What had he been thinking? This would not happen again. Ymir was his home. He would not be going anywhere.

"It is so good to be home. I can't believe that I was gone so long. Forgive me, Jane, for indulging my desire for change and my morbid curiosity for what had happened on Planet Earth," Nicholas moaned and sighed while embracing and kissing his little family.

"I had almost given up hope, but there was part of me that knew that you would make it back – whenever. I kept looking out at that vast star-filled sky above our community and sending you messages. Leia had learned how to call for her Daddy, too."

At that moment, the welcoming committee of humans knocked on the door, waiting to be received. Nicholas greeted his guests and looked carefully at each one as they embraced him and shared kind words. It appeared to him that the men had aged dramatically during his two-year absence. Jordan Kennedy, the retired military officer, had become paunchy and stooped and walked with a limp, while his wife, Ara, had retained her lithe figure and lustrous black hair.

Donald Tracey had become more rotund with faded eyes and hair, and actor Joshua Lipman had retained his handsome face although he looked a little longer in the tooth. Charles Trainor had slipped considerably as his tall frame leaned forward to hear the conversation and to remember where he sat. And what a surprise to see Ernest Hobart leaning on a cane and looking wrinkled and gray. Handshakes that had once been strong and firm were softer and shakier than they had been.

But the women – ah, the women. They were stunning. It seemed that the crevice atmosphere agreed with their skin. Vicky Simmons had retained her young girl look, had lost weight, and developed muscles and a wrinkle-free visage. She looked and sounded sweet and appealing. She and Ara were the youngest members of the original group and could often be seen jogging around the periphery of the community.

Kate Trainer had accumulated a few pounds, but she remained a pretty woman with a strong personality who cared for her ailing husband Charles who would come in and out of reality. Joan Dreyfus had lost weight in her old age but still managed to get around with the aid of a walker. She had become frail but dressed neatly but frumpily, making her look older and more wrinkled.

Her former nemesis, Gladys Henderson, appeared to have aged well with the help of strenuous exercise to ward off osteoporosis since she was a petite, small-boned woman with dyed ash brown hair and upright posture. She and Joan had become more forgiving of one another's character flaws and were able to form a neighborly bond. All the women had adjusted to the limited clothing choices available in Ymir stores.

"Come sit down, Nicholas, and tell us what you found on your trip back to Planet Earth," Kate said as she was eager to hear about her children and grandchildren who had been unable to stay in touch because of the wars.

"Oh yes, yes, do tell us all about it – your space travel and your return to our home. Was it worth your time? Did you meet any of your old colleagues? Were you able to take any pictures?" Donald became excited about the thought of hearing about his family, friends and former community.

Nicholas took a deep breath and tried to find that old controlled commander in chief who had led this motley crew into a new world – one who had coolly promised that they would be here for a few years and then have a happy return home to share their spectacular experiences with family, friends and the media.

Before his departure, he had described only a microscopic picture of what had happened on Earth. He had left out so many details, mainly because he did not know them himself, and he didn't want to alarm them. Now they seemed to have forgotten even the scary details he had told them of what had happened to Planet Earth before he had left for his expedition. It was as if they could recall only the sketchiest picture of the devastation. Nicholas marveled at the capacity of humans to deny and forget.

Yes, parts of the planet had looked like Syria's destruction, but in their version, there were patches of areas with greenery, fields of corn and soybeans and humans working, children playing. Destruction, yes, but all could be repaired and made to look like the original. None of them had experienced nuclear warfare or massive climate changes except through their television sets. They preferred to see it as a series of hurricanes or tsunamis following the blasts and mushroom clouds.

"Show us some pictures, Chief. I am sure you

took pictures when you were there," Jordan requested.

Nicholas wondered whether this former military man wanted his neighbors to know the real truth or whether he, too, had entered the delusional state and made denial a way to cope with reality. Nicholas became dizzy and distraught; and as he stumbled with his words, he promised that after a good night of sleep, he would gather the photos and call a meeting for tomorrow afternoon.

"Right now, let me catch up with you and the news on Ymir. I would love to hear of what has been happening at home."

"Ah yes," Gladys said, "You need to get acquainted with your little girl and re-acquainted with Jane who has been such a stalwart partner and a source of hope for all of us. We will tell you about our lives here later."

"Here, here," the neighbors shouted in unison as they made their way out of the meeting room. "Let's give our fearless commander a little privacy."

"*A domani,* Nicholas, we will return when summoned," Joshua added with an actor's bow and wave.

Chapter 21
Reality Sets in

It was a fitful sleep as Nicholas tossed and turned, trying to block out the images he would be obligated to show his neighbors and his faithful Jane. What would Jane think of what he had to say? She had encouraged him to make the trip, and he thought that she too, was expecting good news and a concrete plan to return to family and friends and start anew. What about little Leia? Would she forever be living in a manufactured crevice community on a distant planet whose air she could not breathe?

As he turned to face Jane, he began to sob and buried his head in his pillow. Jane awoke and embraced him, this formerly totally rational and unemotional enlightenment leader and partner.

"What is it, Nicholas?" What's wrong?" Jane held him close and waited. She knew that she must let him come to her in his own time. Jane had suspected that the trip had been a disaster for him, and she feared that he would never be the same man.

Time seemed to stand still, but finally, Nicholas raised his head and fell helplessly into her arms; and staring into her eyes, he uttered one word, "Hell."

"I can't bear the thought of telling those poor people – my friends – what I learned and saw. No one can even imagine the devastation, the destruction of what was once a beautiful, strange rock in the solar system. I have trouble believing it myself, wondering whether I mistook Earth for a desolate moon."

"Oh, my dearest, it will be difficult for me to hear and see those photos, but we must know the truth so we can accept and embrace our fate," Jane responded, holding back her own tears and rocking back and forth as she cradled Nicholas' head on her quivering shoulder.

"Jane, I can't believe that Earth with its protective ozone shield and its wondrous recycling of carbon could have become a wobbling ball of gray ash. I fear that the new placement will give way to extremes of hot and cold, to solar tempests, to asteroid attacks reminiscent of Earth's early life," Nicholas resorted to a scientific description to manage his feelings.

"What happened to create such chaos? Do we know? Earth was in such a safe location – being far from crowds of stars or supernovae. It seemed as if Planet Earth was in a Goldilocks' zone that made us billions of years away from the black hole in our core," Jane wondered out loud, joining him in an analysis of events.

"Having seen the scorched earth below me, I can only imagine it was self- destructive nuclear wars without end, although it could have been titanic eruptions of several volcanos. I saw no huge holes on the surface indicating asteroids and no signs of alien invasions. Before we left, we knew that a Cold War was heating up again – with potentially more powerful weapons wielded by many more countries with an ax to grind.

"Let's not sugar-coat it for our neighbors. When they see the photos, they will open up that old wound of leaving home yet knowing that Earth had undergone changes keeping them from ever returning there, ever seeing family and friends ever again." Nicholas spoke trying to convince himself that the Humans here on Ymir would see, believe and accept the inevitable. Would some think that these photos were a hoax to keep them on Ymir? Would they lose faith in him as commander and leader?

"Are you ready to have this conversation and show these photos? Prepared for denial, disbelief and despair?" Following a long silence, Jane asked. She tried to prepare him and herself for the worst case scenario and protect her mate while re-assuring herself that she was ready to face the unknown.

"As ready as I'll ever be," Nicholas responded as he collected his equipment and his thoughts. "Is the truth always the best path, Jane?"

"In this case," she answered, "one can't even think of a *good lie*."

Chapter 22
The Awful Truth

The residents had gathered in the main meeting room and had asked the kitchen Robot staff to supply tea, coffee and pastries for the attendees. Little Leia, the favorite 'grandchild' sat in an adjoining room with her robot sitter, Flavia, and had been supplied with chocolate soy milk and munchies. Nicholas and Jane did not want her to see the photos or hear the discussion. Granted she was too young to understand, but they feared that there would be some imprint on her young brain in seeing the photos as well as hearing the responses of the adults, her beloved grandparents, uncles and aunts.

A few of the Browns and Grays who had joined the Ymirian citizenry wanted to hear the Commander and learn about his journey back to his former home. They, too, had escaped from their planet homes to land on Ymir because of violent marauders and had yearned to discover what had happened to their planet and those who had been left behind. They were also curious about Planet Earth's destruction and the effects of his findings had on Nicholas as a leader.

The atmosphere in the room was tense as the Ymirians awaited Nicholas's arrival. The Humans realized that although they knew of the catastrophes on Planet Earth, they held onto the hope that civilization had returned to reclaim the home they had hoped to see again. They had set aside their memories, videos and pictures of what they had left behind and were, only now that Nicholas had returned, willing to recapture those albums of what they had treasured. Jordan held little hope of a positive outcome, but Ara could not bury her enthusiasm for good news – for a rosy picture of a renewed Planet Earth. The others came in and out of their dream-like state, alternating between hope and despair in anticipation.

Nicholas and Jane walked slowly and cautiously into the meeting room and set up the computer so all could easily watch the screen. Nicholas turned to his audience and addressed them in a soft, un-Nicholas-like voice.

"Good morning, fellow Ymirians, What I am about to share with you might be difficult to watch and absorb for you and for me. Please bear with me if I stumble. I am about to show you pictures of what I saw as I circled Planet Earth. My camera and my connections to the few satellites still operating in earth's sky made it possible to get a broad view of the geography and to zone in on particular regions with a closer look. Originally, there had been about 1700 satellites from different countries collecting images and tracking. Some have been destroyed or were not operational."

"What destroyed them? Alien weaponry? Planet Earth militaries?" Jordan asked as he tried to understand the loss of the important communication satellites.

"There were probably many non-military causes, Jordan, asteroids and space debris were often the culprits when I worked for NASA."

"Let me give you a general picture of what could be seen when aerospace engineers and astronomers began mapping our planet." Nicholas switched on the computer and dimmed the lights as he scanned the surface of Planet Earth and the nighttime sky in years past.

A rush of human breath and sighs filled the room as the Earthlings marveled at the beauty of their former home – the greens of forests and grasslands, blues and turquoise of the oceans, golden fields, white snow-capped mountains and earthy tans of deserts swept by their eyes. This is what they had left behind.

Nicholas then switched to other frames, ones he had witnessed on his latest mission. Slowly at first, he allowed them to see the changes in colors; and when he slowed the motion of the camera, he let them see the land masses as they looked now. Gone was the white of the mountain peaks. Gone was the green of the woodlands. Gone was the gold of the fields where humans had planted their crops to feed their people. Gone were the blues of the waters. From afar, the planet had turned into a gray mass of land and a brackish dark brown and black of the rivers and oceans.

"Do you want me to go on? To go closer to the surface while going around the globe?" Nicholas asked in a barely audible voice.

The silence had become unbearable. Soon there were moans sounding like a concerto of sad cellos playing a dirge.

"Yes, go on," they uttered in a chorus.

Nicholas then zoomed in to show them the devastation in the north, the south, the east, the west, the North Pole, Antarctica. Everything was flattened and dark, mountains covered in ash, millions of tons of soot released on the ground and as an aerosol, rivers rushing towards the discolored seas, overflowing the banks and carrying whatever was left of humans, buildings, animals and vegetation. There was no sign of life, nothing but the bleak, graphite landscape and the steely fog and clouds that shrouded everything in gray. Electromagnetic pulses or the bursts of electromagnetic radiation had left any form of communication destroyed.

"How could this have happened, Nicholas, such total and complete desolation?" A continent, yes, but every land mass, every ocean?" Ernest uttered in complete disbelief.

"I have my suspicions but am not sure," Nicholas paused and then continued, "The vast nuclear stockpiles that were unleashed account for some of the destruction." He paused and then continued," but I suspect that the totality was a result of the planet being thrown off its course resulting in a change in atmosphere, in temperature and out of its superior position in the galaxy. Earth became a wind-swept, frozen landscape open to solar tempests that have turned it into an inhospitable, Jupiter-like wobbling planet in the Milky Way galaxy."

"You are saying that no life remains or will never develop, that everything and everyone we knew is no more," Gladys concluded as she wiped the tears from her eyes and held onto Ara's arm.

"I don't know that for sure, Gladys, and that is why I think that we should plan to send a team of robots to return to Earth, gather samples and help us understand. When I was orbiting and on my last lap I thought I saw a greenish-brown patch around the southeastern shore of what I thought was North America. I could not continue to explore because I had deployed the booster rockets to take me out of Earth's orbit."

"What could that be, given that the planet is a frozen mass devoid of life? There probably isn't much oxygen left in the atmosphere given the destruction of the plant life," Joshua asked.

"Why would we put our limited resources to go on a mission to hell when we should be trying to find ways to survive here?" Jordan added in his cold, calculating military analysis voice

"If there is any chance that some one or some group is still alive in a bunker somewhere, wouldn't we want to find and save them?" Kate answered with a tenderness that amazed the group.

"Fat chance for that, Kate. This expedition would be an act of sheer folly in my opinion,"

Ernest spoke in his old way of condescension and disdain.

"There is one reason why we would do this. If my hunch is correct, and that is that our planet has been thrown off course and become uninhabitable, I wonder if another nearby planet, like Mars, wobbled too, and had become the Goldilocks of our solar system," Nicholas offered in his usual customary scientific rationale – leaving his audience in awe and Jane to offer, "Could there be hope for a return to something like our old planet– a good substitute?"

"Is this a hint of things to come," Kate wondered out loud.

Chapter 23
Robots as Explorers

Having agreed, following long and spirited discussions by all Ymirians, that an exploratory mission should be conducted, Nicholas and his team of Grays and robots began to fashion a new type of bots. These small swarming robots would be able to resist extreme radiation and be equipped with specialized radar dirt-proof lenses that could cut through the gray dust and fog of the atmosphere surrounding Planet Earth and record 3-D images.

The arms of the robot would be able to scoop up particles, suck them into internal bags. Hopefully some of their samples would contain DNA of plants, animals and humans that had existed. Should they find any sign of human life, they could land and deploy wheels that would kick up the ash and move slowly along the barren landscape utilizing a shrill whistling sound. And then, if they found life, what next?

That possibility remained a mystery for the moment. The Ymirians thought about the practical actions robots could perform. The global positioning system devices, working with roving satellites remaining above earth would be able to get data about the changes in the rotation of the planet and perhaps determine the causes of Earth's demise.

"Let's try to build and deploy about 200 of these devices and plan their arrival for daytime," Nicholas proposed.

The shrouded Browns responded on their pads, *"200 was too many for the current robot engineers and us to produce and for our 3-D printers on Ymir to replicate. In addition, such a large number would deplete our raw materials."*

"What do you suggest?" Nicholas asked.

"We think 50 would be sufficient for exploration of that planet. Meanwhile we can send our scouts out on Ymir to find other metals we could use to print out more and improved prototypes for this mission and for the next venture into the Milky Way galaxy to find a suitable planet for us to move to in the future should the need arise."

"Where do you shrouded ones hide all those brains hidden in those soft cloaks? You make a lot of sense. I had not thought that far ahead. I wonder if my brain didn't shrink with all that space travel," Nicholas responded with a nod of his head and a step towards the Browns. He stopped and stepped back realizing that he could not shake their hands or offer a comradery embrace. As far as he knew, no one had connected physically with the shrouded ones.

"Now that is something to consider for survival," he mumbled to himself.

"Don't even think of it, Commander, we are

happy with who we are and are not attracted to you earthlings. It's better to isolate our genetic pool. We all have our strengths and weaknesses." The leader communicated in a way that alerted Nicholas to the possibility that the shrouded ones could read what he was thinking. The writing on the pad might only be a secondary communication tool.

"I'll be damned, we Earthlings are not as advanced as we imagined we were," Nicholas thought to himself. Now he was beginning to wonder about these shrouded beings – what did they look like under those garments and how did they reproduce? Where had they come from? What had happened to their home planet?

"All in due time, Commander Nicholas, you have taken your time to think about us or even wonder about our history or our anatomy. Because our different species are so dependent on each other, we are learning to trust one another and becoming more comfortable with sharing." Another text appeared on the pad of some other shrouded one as Nicholas sought to understand what had just happened.

"Right, and we have not been creating weapons of mass destruction or arming and killing one another. Perhaps we here on Ymir share the same value system. What about adding some down time at the end of the workday so we can gather and share stories?" Nicholas suddenly realized that the 'others' had been segregated from the Earthlings – each in their own little silos. They had been enlisted as coworkers but not as fellow citizens of Ymir.

"We will confer with the rest of our clans and let you know," the leader of the Grays who had quietly mingled, responded as the Browns shuffled in their shrouds in agreement.

"Sometimes tragedy brings out the best in creatures, and the universe expands," Nicholas spoke in a reflective, somewhat spiritual tone, "We have been too wedded to our own kind to view your clans as equals and part of the living experience. Perhaps there is something to this Intelligent Designer Myth – a superior being that binds us all together."

"We believe there is no limit to the creativity of a creator should there be one and only one. Ultimately all we can say is that diversity is probably spread throughout all galaxies, and we embrace it to survive."

"I would guess that we may never know the totality of the universe, and to wonder is to keep curiosity and our own creative spirit alive." Nicholas shook his head and bid his neighbors good night as he took the long route back to his home and his family. He had plenty to think about, but he wished he knew how to keep his thoughts to himself, tucked away from the mind readers

Chapter 24
Getting to Know You

Nicholas immediately went to work on fulfilling his promise to recognize and learn more about the Brown and Gray hooded figures. It was as if a light bulb had gone off in his brain, and now he was a man on a mission. He would confer with Jane who was so level-headed and in possession of the social skills and winsome personality that he lacked. She also would know the ways of the community and how to get the dialogue going among such disparate players.

He had been working with the Browns in the design workshop attempting to get the best possible drone-type robot to accomplish the mission. The twenty shrouded ones and Nicholas had put forth several possible designs: flat ones with lowering caterpillar wheels, tall ones that looked like pyramids and round ones that could bounce around the surface of the planet should that become necessary. They all needed a break from the brain work.

Nicholas wrote on the pad. "Time out for today. Sleep on it if you do indeed do that kind of thing and dream about more possibilities for tomorrow."

"Sweet dreams, Commander Nicholas. For your information – we do engage in rest and sleep."

Nicholas chuckled and hurried back to find Jane and Leia who were playing on a small swing he had built for his daughter. He looked upon the scene with great joy and satisfaction. Ever since returning from his fateful trip to Planet Earth, he had become a more human Earthling by becoming more willing to admit to the feelings and thoughts of Everyman. Who knew that a loving partner and a little girl could transform him from an unemotional creature into a doting parent and dependent spouse.

"Hey, my lovelies, what have you been up to today?" he said as he picked up Leia in his arms and twirled her around until she squealed with delight. He set her down on the swing and sat by Jane, embracing her and whispering in her ear.

"You have no idea how much I love you and how happy I am to be home."

"My, my, if I had known what a little space flight would do to make you into a perfect man, I would have sent you out sooner," Jane teased.

"What a day I have had. First of all, my team never ceases to surprise me. Those Browns are not only brilliant engineers, but they have powers to astound and astonish."

"Like what?" Jane responded with a curious smile.

Nicholas, looking serious and subdued, answered with a lowered voice and a lean in to Jane's ear, "I think they can read our minds."

"Silly man, I have known that for a long time. I noticed that while you were away and could not communicate with us, but they would come to me and tell me where you were. They would write on their pads in ways that told me that they could tell what was going through your mind when you were circumventing Earth. They are not creative writers normally, but with you at the helm, they could wax poetical," Jane said as she began to explain how she unraveled their secret.

"That confirms it and tells me that we must learn more about our shrouded neighbors and coworkers because we have been so disinterested in them as fellow travelers – I can't say people, can I?" Nicholas asked with a perplexed look on his face.

"Nicholas, they are people but people from other planets. Sometimes, you are so narrow in your thinking. You have a fixed point in your mind when you say people and exclude others because they don't look like you or are unfamiliar," Jane said in compassionate frustration.

"I know. I know. I realize that I am quite rigid about so many things. I understood today that we Earthlings must expand our views even more than we have. I have always marveled at the way we allowed such different beings – people – into our community and into our lives." Nicholas was becoming more and more animated and chatty.

"We have been more interested in what they could do for us or how they could help us than who they were, where they came from and what they really looked like under those robes. We have been underestimating and treated them somewhat as our ancestors did with the slaves."

"Don't forget, Nicholas, that they also needed us when they were being attacked, and the Browns did drop their cloaks for a moment to allow us to get a glimpse of them. But I agree that we have not fully integrated them into our community as brothers and sisters of this universe. How are we going to change that?" Jane's mind was traveling along the same channel as Nicholas' and she now began to catch his fervor.

"What do you think about getting our group together with a similar number of Browns and Grays and begin to explore our differences and commonalities?" Nicholas was ready to plunge right in and get to the core of the issues.

"I'm not sure that jumping so quickly and directly is the way to go. Let's just start with social hours for some of the Earthlings and an equal number of the others. There would be less emphasis on us as the leaders and them as guests. They could choose among their groups, and we could do the same. Every week we would hold one of these social hours, but print up a schedule for other meetings and have sign ups. The only framework would revolve around the meeting time, the numbers of each group, and the presence of either you or me to facilitate," Jane offered her plan to her beaming husband who sat closer to her and congratulated her on her brilliance.

"Let's do it," Nicholas answered quickly and

then proceeded to do his commander thing. "You can set this up in the next few days, and then we can communicate our ideas to the groups."

Jane chuckled and poked Nicholas saying, "You give birth to the greatest ideas and...."

Nicholas interrupted, "Right, and you polish and perfect and then put them into action. What a team!"

Chapter 25
The First Foray into the Unknown

"Come on in," Jane said, as she welcomed Gladys, Ernest, Ara and Joshua into the main meeting room where twenty chairs had been placed in a circle with snack tables nearby. The lighting was soft and generous to the guests as they awaited their neighbors.

"Do we know who is coming from the community?" Gladys asked.

"All I know is that a representative group from the Browns will be attending, but I don't know the specifics. Remember that you must use your pads to respond to their writing. You can speak, but the voice will be translated on your and their pads. It will be a bit of a challenge to convert from voice to written word when you are conversing, but we'll get the hang of it," Jane said as she spoke in her most re-assuring voice.

As she spoke, she heard a rustling of fabric as six Browns came in and greeted their neighbors with a lifting of their shrouds. They came as a group and sat near each other in the circle.

Jane welcomed them with her written words and then invited everyone to help themselves to the beverages placed on the tables near their chairs. Water bottles with metal straws had been provided, and all but the Brown Ones partook of the drink at the beginning of the session.

Jane began by sharing the focus of these meetings and the hopeful outcome for all the different inhabitants of Ymir.

"Commander Nicholas and I thought that it was time to really get to know one another as neighbors, coworkers and friends since it looks like we will be here for a while or maybe forever. Anyone can share anything about themselves, their origins, culture – whatever you think would help in forging a true community."

"Let me start, Jane, because I am not sure that everyone knows about our history and why we came to this planet in the first place," Gladys began and seeing the nodding heads of her neighbors and the movement of the shrouded ones, she decided to go on with her speech. She spoke slowly and clearly.

"We came from Planet Earth in the Milky Way Galaxy as an experimental team led by Commander Nicholas with the goal of finding out what would be the results of having older Earthlings explore a new way of living on Ymir. Our space agency, NASA, was interested in studying the effects of space travel and how living on another world would change us physically, socially and psychologically. We had known each other on Earth since we lived in the same building, but we were not close nor friendly - only neighbors"

Ernest interrupted, "Yes, and we were supposed to stay here a few years and then return home."

Joshua added, "We could not return home. Our planet was no longer livable because of nuclear devastation initiated by warring tribes of our species and the ensuing disastrous climate changes. All was lost, and so here we are on Ymir – living in a crevice community created to keep us alive."

"And thanks to you and others, we are living well," Ara spoke, directing her gaze at the Browns.

Everyone turned to look at their pads to await a response. Silence, rustling and then a ding indicating that someone was writing.

"Thank you, and you are aware that we found refuge in your community. This routing was the second time we were driven from our homes. Initially we lived on a distant moon of Saturn that had been hospitable to living beings when it had cooled down from elemental fire. It continued to cool until the temperature was just right to establish soil that harbored brown, grass-like plants and perhaps some early living forms. For thousands of years, sentient beings evolved together with edible materials that flourished in an atmosphere rich in a gas that allowed us to utilize it to stay alive. I believe you call this gas, carbon dioxide.

"Our tribe flourished and became able to build, develop language and reproduce ourselves when our structures began to deteriorate. Over thousands of years, we had a rich civilization built on what you would call intelligence. Our lifespan was

extending to a thousand years."

"And then what happened?" Ernest wrote in his own hurried, demanding way.

"The atmosphere began changing, becoming colder and more inhospitable," wrote the leader of the Browns. *"We had to find a way to survive. We chose a group of about 100 able-bodied, younger beings who could still reproduce asexually and convinced them to leave the rest of us behind and find a new planet for them and perhaps all of us, to inhabit. We gave them the means to remain connected to our gaseous atmosphere through a process of recycling the carbon and sent them out in one of our space crafts."*

"And you, I take it, were one of the able-bodied who led the expedition." Gladys wrote as she sat in wide-eyed wonder.

"Yes, I was in a position similar to Commander Nicholas due to my past experience in locating a possible new home and developing the pads we use to communicate with others. I have excellent hearing and language abilities, but my fellow Browns have extraordinary gifts that help us survive in many different habitats."

"You said that you reproduce asexually. How does that happen and doesn't that mean you don't have much variation?" Ara asked, demonstrating her knowledge of biology.

"We have been reproducing ourselves in various ways over time. During our evolution, we have used binary fission when we were simple multicellular beings. This was followed by 'budding' where-

by a polyp would break off from the parent and develop into a new being. Then we developed the ability to reproduce sexually, but under certain conditions. We can also multiply by parthenogenesis whereby a polar body develops and fertilizes the female part called the egg."

"Do you mean that you now have a variety of means of reproduction?" Gladys asked.

"Right. Under stress we can revert to budding to preserve our genetic integrity and our energy," the biologist in the group wrote.

Joshua wrote hurriedly in order to get to his most important question, "So what do you look like under those Robes?"

"We think it would be wiser for us to reveal our body structure when we are all together as a community so we are all on the same page and in similar states. We did lower our robes once when we were installing the solar panels, but I doubt you would remember since the event was erased from your consciousness."

The conversation went on for another hour with questions and answers being exchanged for both the Earthlings and the shrouded ones. There were surprises and gasps on both sides as the neighbors tried to understand and visualize the essence of the other – the anatomy, the physiology, the 'brain', the thinking and the culture. Finally they all agreed that the process would be much easier if they could communicate directly in the same language.

"We are not there yet, but The Grays and the

Browns have been working on this in our community and in our spare time. We might have some results for you soon. Meanwhile, we could help you Earthlings learn to mind read," the leader of the Browns known as Brown1X responded as the Humans continued to express wonderment and awe.

Chapter 26
Getting to Know You, Too

Gathered together in the meeting room, Jordan, Vicky, Donald, Kate and Joan looked apprehensive and pensive as they awaited the representatives of the Gray Ones. They spoke to each other in quiet voices and tried to reassure themselves that this meeting would go as well as the one held with the Brown Ones. They had so many questions to ask, but they had been advised to be patient and open to listening to the fractured voices wearing the gray shrouds.

Jane entered and led a group of ten of the Grays with the blackish/gray hoods who followed. They joined the Earthlings in the circle and nodded to greet their neighbors as the soft folds moved around the top of their figures.

"Welcome, everyone. Thank you for coming here tonight. Since you all know the reasons for our get together, I won't repeat the introduction, but I will ask about the extent of your knowledge. What do you know about the reason for the Earthlings' trip to Ymir?"

One of the Grays leaned in and spoke in a raspy voice, *"We ve learn that your plan et was destr oyed follo ing your arriv al on Ymr,"* a voice *from inside the top of the shroud translated.*

The voice came as a surprise to the Humans, but they ignored the change for fear of antagonizing the Grays. They were possibly trying a new way to communicate.

"Yes, and we came here as part of a research study by our Space Agency, NASA, to study the effects of space travel and existence on another planet on older humans. We were only supposed to be here for a few years," Jordan responded to the opening salvo.

A second Gray One opened the top of his robe to expose a protrusion coming from a neck-like structure. A long finger-like, gray pencil extended out from a knob at the end of an appendage. It adjusted the lit areas of the box, withdrew all this apparatus into the robe and said, *"We, too, were driven from our planet which was close to Planet Earth in the same galaxy. I believe you called it Pluto. The seismic disturbances in our galaxy forced some of us to flee from the Milky Way to find safety."*

"I thought Pluto was considered a moon and not a planet. How did you live on that desolate place?" Joan asked.

"Since we do not have lungs, we don't need oxygen or any other gas to be alive. We are a self-contained, closed system and recycle all we need. We are also able to transform ourselves into other types of beings as some of us here on Ymir want to look like the humans so we are working on becoming replicants."

"Do you mean that soon some of you will become humans?" Joan asked as she gasped for air.

"Yes and no. We will look like you but retain our basic system. We can live along side you but by no means seek to mate with you or behave as you do."

"Speaking of mating, how do you increase the number of your kind?" Joan asked without utilizing her finely tuned filter.

"We have a special part of our system set aside for budding. A lump forms, grows and breaks off into a smaller version of the original host that slowly transforms into an 'adult' who then joins our tribe. We also have other means to insure that our beings can survive."

"No sex, no pleasure," Donald interrupted while winking and smiling at Jordan who maintained a straight-laced military stance.

"And no childbirth pain!" Joan adds. "How marvelous!"

"How will we be able to distinguish you from us?" Jordan asked with justifiable curiosity.

"We are bioengineered forms able to transform ourselves back to our original structure. We are programmed to be peaceful and helpful to other life systems. Our transformational abilities are our only defense as of now, but the program could be changed to produce a more aggressive replicant should the need arise. Right now we have become experts in computer language, communication, design and becoming gladiators sworn to build and protect. We are the ones who have made things happen in response to the ingenuity of Browns and

you Earthlings."

"You need not fear this small group of humans. We are a peaceful lot in addition to being too old to fight," Donald quipped.

"We would not be able to say that about some of our former citizens. Many were always ready to turn violent against someone different. They saw danger everywhere leading to anxiety in people and to endless struggles and wars," Vicky added her negative spin to the conversation as all the humans nodded in agreement.

Jane looked at the circle of different life forms behaving as neighbors in conversation and thought that it was time to have closure.

"This has been a wonderful experience for me, friends. I hope our discussions will continue because we have to formulate a plan for all of us to find a safer place to live in peace and harmony if the need arises. As you know the intruders are at our gates. This will be a time for unity and resolve, but we as a community have so many gifts that I doubt we will fail."

Different sounds of approval, rustling of robes and clapping of hands and appendages rose from the audience as Jane moved to end the meeting and return triumphantly to Nicholas and Leia.

"What a wonderful meeting, Nicholas. Everyone was friendly and curious about each other, and we were all having a good time laughing and showing some humor about our differences."

"It couldn't have come at a better time because we will have to work as a team to quicken the pace of our mission to find a safer planet. While you were meeting, the Guardian robots repelled a brutal attack from marauding invaders; but the reports show that these attacks are becoming fiercer and more dangerous. It is time for us to *get out of Dodge.*"

Chapter 27
The Robot Explorers

The robot laboratory was buzzing with activity as the chief Human, his mate, Jane, and a select group from the Browns and Grays met each day to design robots that could be sent out into the universe to find a planet that could sustain this motley crew of space travelers. Programs to explore planets within the Milky Way and exoplanets further away would have to be explored for habitability. While some of the possibilities were described by scientists on Earth, most had been catalogued by the Grays' scientists.

Robots would be utilizing HARPS (the High Accuracy Radial Velocity Planet Searcher) which would be retrieved from Commander Nicholas who had worked on the project utilizing this technique while helping to develop the Kepler space telescope on Planet Earth. The Grays had developed long range telescopes and micro-lensing, a form of gravitational lensing utilizing light bending in background and foreground lenses, to create images. Combining these techniques in one type of robot would require technology not available on Ymir. The striped brown and gray Explorer robots would utilize different technologies and would be designed to travel to different parts of the galaxies.

Production levels were limited, but the team was able to program seventy-five robots that would be launched into space while recording data to be analyzed upon return to Ymir. No one expected all to return to home base since radiation and gravitational pull from the stars in various galaxies might destroy the group or at least 50% of the robots. Algorithms developed by the Grays had predicted this outcome. Despite these frightening figures, the teams decided to deploy this scouting team of explorers.

On the day of the launching, expectations were high. The robots would be loaded onto three rockets, each aimed at different parts of the sky with programmed instructions on where to explore. The robots would then travel until a planetary orbit captured them. As they circumnavigated the exoplanets in the outer galaxies or planets in the Milky Way, the robots would conduct the tests designed to determine if there was water or if the atmosphere was conducive to life. Others would travel to other galaxies faintly identified but laden with possibilities.

"It's as if we are sending our kids off to college, Jane. I feel apprehensive about this launch," Nicholas told Jane as he paced around the area near the launch pad wearing his space suit and oxygenated helmet.

"I think you might be feeling envious because

you want to go on this mission. Remember you are not a robot," she responded, as she affectionately punched his padded arm and stood up on her tippy toes to stare through the visor into his blue eyes.

"Maybe there is a little of that, but basically I fear that these robots will be space dust, and we won't be able to find a new home. I don't want our daughter to live out her life in a crevice – no matter how well appointed it is. Our community is a fantasy land and not sustainable in addition to being vulnerable to attackers living on the surface."

"We lived in a fantasy land back home with so many conflicting views, such as inequalities in our culture, and so little strong leadership. We could not keep ourselves from polluting our home and our food, from killing each other and from an 'I got mine, I win, you lose' attitude. At least we get along here on Ymir."

"What is the future here, Jane? It looks bleak to me."

"Perhaps we have to focus on the present, to understand that we are finite creatures and that we have a beginning and an end," Jane responded in a philosophical tone.

"I am not willing to accept that finite end. I agree with the futurists like Ray Kurzwell who liked to push the boundaries of technology and human existence. I read about those prognosticators on Earth who were working on making death irrelevant, to eradicate disease and to constantly renew and remake humanity with the inevitable growth of singularity."

"Well, you know me, Nicholas, I cannot envision this coming technological explosion and a certain singularity. It's fun to have these futuristic fantasies where we imagine great future events, but it's just been fairy dust sprinkled on unsuspecting readers, especially techies. I believe in human agency, and now I believe in creature agency, not some autonomous computer life form," Jane said in a firm, no nonsense manner that left Nicholas dumbfounded.

At that point, the Browns had launched the rockets, and the Ymirians watched as the the space vehicles veered in three directions – one towards the Orion arm of the Milky Way and Planet Earth to check on survivors or any sign that life could be restored – one towards the spur of the Milky Way which would then explore the other arms of the spiral galaxy – and one that would travel beyond the Milky Way to find its way to the extragalactic part of the universe, perhaps the Andromeda galaxy or beyond.

There was no elation among the Humans, Browns or Grays. They had sent their hopes and dreams onto those three rockets and those robots. They were spent.

"What will be, will be," Jane told Nicholas as she pulled him towards home.

Chapter 28
Who Was Left Behind?

Robots in Team E had been orbiting Planet Earth for what seemed like an eternity but was only several days in Earthling time when one robot spotted a greenish-brown spot and what seemed to be an unusual patch of color amid the surrounding gray near the southern coast of Florida. Closer inspection with extra sensitive telescopic lenses revealed a space that could not have been more than one mile in diameter overlooking what once was the bluish Atlantic Ocean.

One of the robots made circular trips around the spot and finally made a soft landing near what looked like a cave abutting a low lying rocky mass. Its rotating camera circled the area for signs of life and its soft whizzing sound broke the stony silence of the desolated planet. A stooped figure appeared from the cave entrance followed by a mangy dog that at one time would have been called a Golden Retriever. The white-haired, ashen man with faded blue eyes, long fingernails protruding from thin emaciated arms slowly approached the robot E1.

"I am a survivor of the destruction of Planet

Earth, and I have written a report detailing my observations and memories of this catastrophe. It is rolled up in this tubing I found washed up on the shore. If you are from another planet, you can take it with you and show the humans who may still be alive out there. I don't know if you understand me, but I hope you can deliver this."

The robot extended one of its arms to retrieve it from the survivor who then slowly turned and walked back into the darkened cave area where there would be quiet and comfort until he could re-energize himself to walk out to the green area where his meal would be growing in the radioactive atmosphere.

Using the special light sensors to resume its travels, Team E rose from the patch and lifted into the poisoned atmosphere and back into space. The team had accomplished its mission and had been programmed to return to Ymir to deliver its cargo. Traveling with repetitive bursts of light energy, two of Team E arrived on Ymir while other fellow robot travelers continued their search for new homes in the galaxies.

Nicholas had begun to receive signals once Team E entered the space around Ymir. He guided the two robots down to a soft landing and joined Gray OneX, affectionately known as Joe, in approaching the still-spinning robot group. Once the two came to a complete rest, Nicholas and Joe examined the structures for signs of wear and tear while removing the computer chips that would be analyzed in the Grays' lab. Thinking that they had completed the inspection, Nicholas noted an extra piece of metal in the extension arm of one of the robots.

He carefully removed it and showed it to Joe who appeared puzzled by the contents of what he thought was a leaf of some kind. Nicholas wrote on his pad, 'Paper' – from trees that had populated Planet Earth. Joe pointed to the blackish scribbles on the paper. Nicholas wrote, 'Language.' Joe had already deciphered the writing but allowed Nicholas to read and explain, "This is terrible, Joe. It is the final nail in the coffin. Let's examine the computer chips for the photographs that will most likely confirm Givens' account and then share with our community."

Having checked out the damning photos they walked to the central meeting room, calling the teams to stop working and attend a meeting to hear the latest news from home. The community gathered to hear Nicholas read the epistle from Planet Earth. He explained the circumstances under which the news had reached Ymir and then began to read from a crumpled sheet of water-stained paper:

"I am a survivor of the dark night and days where the crazy leaders of this planet unleashed a series of actions that would result in Planet Earth becoming Planet Ash. Let me tell you my version of what I think happened based on news accounts leading up to wars between nations and Mother Nature's responses to the unfolding events lasting about four years. Our country, The United States of

America, and many others had succumbed to the propaganda denouncing the status quo and the ruling elite. The citizens, who had been displaced by technologically shifting industrial production in the globalized economy and a loss of jobs, joined the nouveau riche of the business country club set and set in motion the events that would lead to the election of a politically inexperienced person who had been part of the pop culture scene and knew how to get attention to his messages by utilizing the media and the social network organizations. His calls to drain the swamp resonated with many Americans but resulted in more division and disaffection. He surrounded himself with men and women who carried out the leaders' policies because they knew they were right and would make their country great again. That nationalistic fever grew and spread throughout the United States and other nations worldwide.

This political movement that had been seen before in the twentieth century, spread like contagion across the planet and resulted in rancor, genocides, wars, cultural upheavals and finally in atomic warfare. Many nations developed dirty bombs and threatened their neighbors. Dictators flourished as citizens wanted strong leaders who would protect them. The United Nations disintegrated as no one trusted the organization and stopped funding its programs. Racism, misogyny, and fanaticism grew and horrendous atrocities occurred in the name of security.

Instead of focusing on the changes occurring in

the climate and the increasing disasters from flood-ing, volcanic eruptions, fires and sudden changes in temperature all over the globe, the leaders denied that Mother Nature was unleashing havoc and re-fused to address the issues plaguing the planet.

I don't know how I survived, but I suspect that since I was scuba diving with the newest state-of-the-art mixed gas and re-breathing gear and my pouch, I avoided the immediacy of the blasts taking place in the States and I assume, the planet. I was swept ashore and found myself in this cave togeth-er with Fido. I have been living on the remaining grasses outside the cave and the few fish I can catch. I don't expect to find other survivors, at least not anywhere near me, and I am too weak to walk to explore. It won't be long before Fido and I join the others in death.

Jeffrey Givens
Deep Sea Explorer and Biologist

That news and the new photos confirmed what Nicholas had reported to the neighbors up-on his return. Now the absolute destruction re-ported by this lonely survivor extinguished any glimmer of hope for a return trip back to Planet Earth. That planet was no longer home.

Jane lowered her eyes and ended the evening, "Goodbyes hurt so much when the story was not finished, but now, the good-bye is the end."

Chapter 29
The Robots Find a Place

Teams MW (Milky Way), and EG (Extra Galactic) had not completed their missions, but the Ymirians anxiously awaited their return, especially now that more marauding groups had been attempting to invade the crevice. These groups had been repelled, but at a cost of Gray life forms and the destruction of robots, defenders of the entrances. It was imperative that a new home planet be found as soon as possible. Without an exit strategy and an escape, it was only a matter of time before the Ymirians would be destroyed.

Finding their way around the more than three thousand planets in the Milky Way galaxy and finding exoplanets in galaxies 3.8 billion light years away was going to take time and attention to the limiting technology of microlensing. Spotting the distant quasar galaxy RXJ1131-1231 had been a victory for Earth's astronomers, but they were able to do no more than collect a few images of the light distortions. No telescope had been developed to view evidence of life. Explorer robots perhaps could get closer and identify any sign of water or organic matter.

Finally, Team MW returned to Ymir with evidence that there were several planets that were probably habitable. The most promising was a Kepler452B that had been discovered previously by astronomers on Earth. Further examination of the recorded data showed evidence of water and amino acids. The atmosphere was composed of some oxygen, some evidence of ash, ice crystals and metal vapor. Hydrogen had been evaporating from the planet, and a magnetic field was detected.

"This looks like a strong possibility for us," Commander Nicholas told his team.

Joe nodded, *"I agree with you, and we should not waste any time exploring it further and upgrading our space capsules and building new ones. The hordes are at the gates."*

"What about the other teams out there exploring extragalactic space? Do we want to discount what they might bring?" Jordan Kennedy asked.

"Hopefully, they will return while we are here in preparation," Jane responded as she sought justification for her cursory response.

"We can also re-program them to follow us to our new home if they are on the return flight and then utilize their data for possible future moves to newer homes in the future," Joe said. *"This constant migration may be the new normal, I fear."*

Ignoring Joe's dire prediction, Nicholas re-assumed command.

"Looks like we are all on the same page," Nicholas stated in his matter-of fact way, "Let's get to work on those space capsules while Joe and his team explore Kepler452B."

Jordan nodded his head in agreement and vowed to call a meeting of the community to let them know that all Ymirians were about to emigrate to another planet to avoid violence and destruction of their home. There would be no repetition of Planet Earth's devastation from nuclear wars and tribal conflicts, he thought to himself.

Following the meeting of the Earthlings and the orders given to the Grays and the Browns by the leadership team, the members of each group accepted the decision with quiet compliance,

Working groups began to meet in different locations, each with a specific goal. Humans and Grays worked to brainstorm and develop options. The team with Nicholas, Joe and Brown1X began to envision a combination of a temporary structure that would mimic the atmosphere of Ymir's crevice while they planned for the terraforming of the land mass to support plant and unicellular life. This idea, envisioned by Carl Sagan, looked at seeding the land elements with micro-algae to accommodate the oxygen needs of the future inhabitants. While this manipulation of the Kepler452B surface was being developed, the robots would carry parts of Ymir to the new home allowing the Ymirians to live in a giant dome-like structure to accommodate their survival while their planet was being bio-engineered.

It was a grand plan that would take time and materials yet to be developed. Rockets and space capsules repaired or built from scratch. Food supplies would have to be harvested from the greenhouses on Ymir or on storage shelves and packaged to fit into the space ships. While the advance robots that had been dispatched earlier built the dome according to the team's instructions, the Ymirians would suspend their metabolism and hibernate in their space capsules while in travel or following the landing, thereby saving energy and setting aside their fears and doubts.

All hands were on board; Humans, Grays, Browns and robots seemed to be programmed to act as one. The females of Homo Sapiens worked alongside their male counterparts and their 'different' neighbors as if they were equal partners committed to one goal – getting ready to find a new home before the destruction of their crevice community by the outliers who were 'storming the ramparts.'

"I don't know how this is going to turn out for us, but it surely feels good to have a mission," Donald told the group. His neighbors nodded in agreement.

The older women, Gladys and Joan, were put in charge of supplies and distribution. They whispered to each other that they were at the bottom of the organizational chart, but they agreed that disputing this here and now would have no effect. They fumed in silence but dove into their work. Kate and Ara worked together to connect the manufactured pieces according to the plan outlined by the design team. Vicky was project coordinator who kept after the teams to insure that there was no slacking off and no negativity floating around all work sites.

Ernest chimed in with his positive/negative vibe assuring his neighbors that no matter what happened, the effort would have been worth it, "Nothing ventured, nothing gained."

All of this activity and stimulation appeared to have given the humans a new lease on life. There was a sprightly spring in their steps, their appetites improved, and they reported that they slept all through the night. Joan had expected to end her life on Ymir once she learned of Earth's demise; but she rallied and found a new meaning in her life, one that involved helping others in a way she had never done before. Empathy had entered her aging brain. Her neighbors responded to this new Joan with hesitancy at first, but they soon warmed up to her while she was on this path.

Gladys was even more energetic and positive as she scurried around doing what she could to help the teams. She had begun to wonder whether she could live far beyond her eighty-two years since she felt so young and strong. Was there something that changed in her DNA or was it just the thrill of adventure? Would she lose her vitality once they arrived at their new home? She did not understand the physics of time and space, but she had a suspicion that something had changed her and her neighbors. Nature? Nurture? Something the Browns or Grays did without her knowing? The universe's doing?

"Commander Nicholas, what has been going

on with us?" Gladys inquired.

"For the last few months, I have noticed a change in our group, including you and Jane. The men have become more light-hearted and gentle with each other and all of the members of the community. I swear that I think some of them have grown hair on their formerly bald heads."

Nicholas chuckled and brushed back his curly locks and gave his beard a quick brush, "You know, Gladys, you might be on to something because I have been observing the changes in Jane. She seems to be shedding that middle-age chunkiness and has become more svelte with her formerly darker hair becoming more golden. She also has more energy and youthful interest than she had when I first returned from my trip."

"Better check out the others, too, because the physical and psychological changes have been surprising to me. We did get along better when we were under siege, but this is different. Look at that old curmudgeon, Ernest. He is now charming and bearable."

"Yes, you're right, and Charles seems less likely to forget things and get lost while walking in the yard outside the compound. I think I will bring this up to Joe and the other newer arrivals."

"But don't forget to include Jordan because he is the only one who does not seem to have changed for the better or worse. He remains the same," Gladys added to insure that she had not forgotten anyone.

"Another mystery to be solved in good time.

Right now our goal is to build and move as quickly as we safely can, Gladys; but I won't forget." Nicholas had become more convinced that time was of the essence, and that he must be firm in his mission to lead his neighbors to safety. If the Browns and Grays were manipulating our genes or our minds, then so be it. Mutations or engineering of our brains are better than annihilations.

Chapter 30
The Voyage and the Arrival

The coordinated work of all inhabitants of Ymir – Humans, Browns, Grays, all manner of robot teams – and the constant threats at the surface led to an early development of all of the needed products necessary for the launch. The workers were depleted but ready to rest when traveling to their new home. The launches of the newly developed rocket systems and the three space ships were successful, and the travelers looked wistfully out the windows as they watched Ymir fade into the star-studded blackness.

Time-traveling to Kepler452B had been uneventful since all creatures on board the spacecrafts were in a state of suspension with a low metabolic rate and a sleep-like condition. No one moved around in zero gravity resulting in a stillness inside the capsules. No one was looking out at the shooting stars, the asteroids whizzing by or the planets boasting of their beauty. The robots in the other two space ships lay dormant awaiting to be re-programmed and put into action

Nicholas had manipulated his hibernation to end before the others. As he swirled around the main capsule, he checked each cubby where the

Humans, 25 of the Grays and 25 of the Browns lay in peaceful slumber. Leia was safely bound to Jane and unable to move should she awake. They looked like a portrait of mother and child from a museum on Earth. He sighed and began to utter a wish out loud hoping that he had made the right decision and that his little family would arrive safely.

Duty called and he snapped to attention and headed to the control panel where he found that Joe had preceded him and was busy checking out the coordinates and the possible estimated time of their arrival.

"Well, Joe, I see you are hard at work. Anything out of the ordinary coming our way?" Nicholas wrote as he spoke, keeping all forms of communication open.

"Just a few near misses from those asteroid bodies and some knocks and scrapes from smaller space junk. It looks like others have been in this part of the galaxy. Let's hope they aren't aiming for the same spot we are. We should be there in earth time of sixty-four hours," Joe responded. *"Now what is on your mind, Nicholas? I'm curious about the vibes I'm getting."*

"I should have known that you knew about my conversation with Gladys. She brought up her curiosity about the changes in Earthlings' personalities in the past few months. We were wondering whether you and yours had anything to do with it."

"There has been some interaction between my team and one Earthling who appeared to be de-

sired by one of us – my engineer, who is young and seeking new experiences. I noticed that they were huddling in the corner of the loading dock one evening."

"Really? Who could that have been? Only Vicky is eligible for romance and eager to experience new adventures," Nicholas responded in surprise, "but wouldn't you have mind-read their conversation?"

"We do have a code of ethics in our culture, and we value a right to privacy among ourselves. Having said that, we are also able to block each other's mind reading ability. Only in dire circumstances can that ability be blocked by the majority who may view the block as a threat to the community."

"What could have happened between them?"

"We do have the ability to transfer our genetic material to another being different than we are. You Earthlings call it horizontal genetic transfer, but you had observed it in bacteria. We can create a phage or a virus with a nucleic acid interior surrounded by protein. We can transfer our genetic material. Then the phage can be driven by touch." Joe was speaking in such a matter-of-fact way that Nicholas felt shocked but not frightened.

"In other words, he could have impregnated her in this odd way without having to adjust different parts to combine easily and lead to the same outcome?"

"It may be odd to you earthlings, but it is one of our many ways of insuring our survival. Your main technique may be more suited to your biology, but I

would not label it odd although the process may look strange to us," Joe scolded.

"Oh, I meant no offense. Could this result in a new life form to add to our diversity? Wonder of wonders, this could be the beginning of a new world order with such possibilities of transformation," Nicholas could not stop his mind from spiraling out of control.

"Let's wait and see – and also not let this interfere with our current mission. This kind of event could lead to irrational warfare from those who want to retain the status quo and the purity of their kind." Joe spoke as a wise leader who was grounded and not given to flights of fancy.

"Absolutely, Joe, this will be 'forgotten' until the right time; but tell me if it was possible that you Grays could have found some way to alter personality through genetic manipulation?"

"Don't like what you see, Nicholas? 'Only the Shadow knows' the answer to that question," Joe responded with a shaking motion beneath the robe.

Chapter 31
The Many Faces of Kepler452B

Kepler452B was identified as a planet by Earthling astronomers who described it as being five-times the mass of Earth and that it orbited its star in three hundred eighty-five days. Habitable, as was Earth, and dotted with many active volcanoes and a rocky surface. It had been the topic of conversation among Earth astronomers for many years.

Nicholas had heard of it because of the SETI Group, a group of scientists who searched for Extraterrestrial Intelligence. That group, once housed in California, had not found any evidence for alien radio signals. The Ymirians did not want to believe that it was inhabited by marauding groups but desperately hoped that it had a good chance of surviving as an exoplanet for millions of years to come.

When the Ymirians woke from their suspended animation, they found they had landed on the rocky surface that extended miles from their capsules. Joe and Nicholas had taken control of the spacecraft to insure a safe landing much as Neil Armstrong and Buzz Aldrin had when they landed on the moon. The remaining spacecrafts carrying robots and supplies had landed nearby.

With their helmet gear securely in place, the Ymirians began to explore the area noting the vastness and quiet of their potentially new home. It was sunny and warm outside their suits, but they knew that caution was necessary at the beginning since they had been told that the precise content of the atmosphere was unknown. They were all curious about the place sold as an Eden with oceans and warm breezes to enjoy. The reality was that none of the beauty could be appreciated while living in a giant greenhouse, a domed structure that would be their home for years to come while they waited for the agricultural sustaining soil to bear fruit and ultimately mutate to thrive in the low oxygen atmosphere.

Once again the Earthlings and their neighbors walked towards their new home with curiosity, excitement and fear. Jordan remained detached and observant while holding Ara's trembling hand. All hoped for a perhaps – perhaps, this new home would be their last attempt to find peace and safety.

They shuffled along, grasping each other's gloved hands while silently uttering prayers and exhortations. The Grays and Browns advanced with stoic determination while harboring doubtful thoughts and carefully programmed hypervigilance.

Only Vicky marched ahead with enthusiasm and energy, and she thought to herself, *She had hidden her secret cargo from her neighbors, but she knew that the time would come when she could no longer avoid the inevitable.*

"I will share when we have all settled in our new home. I can only guess at the reactions – Gladys and Joan will be fine with it while Jordan and Ara will be shocked and dismissive. The others could go either way. We will have to wait and see," she pondered as she tried to convince herself that she and her young lover would live happily ever after.

"Oh my," yelled Gladys as she found herself staring at a huge transparent structure looming in the distance. "This looks like something from a Spielberg movie set with a magical feel. Is this our new home, Commander Nicholas?"

"It surely looks like the design we settled on and programmed the robots to start building before we left Ymir. It's functional but perhaps not aesthetic. What do you think?" Nicholas was amazed himself at the size of the structure and its plastic clarity that rose above the planet floor in organic majesty.

"Won't everyone on the outside see what we are doing during the day?" Kate asked as she struggled to get her mind around the immenseness and visibility of their new home.

Joe looked at the Earthlings and wondered how these creatures managed to exist so long given their extreme emotionality. *"This is like a giant football stadium with a retractable roof. We will need the star's light and heat, but we can hide it at will."*

"Let's get inside the dome and see what has

been built so far. We will need to retrofit the space capsules as soon as possible to allow for the remaining Browns, Grays and robots on Ymir to join us. We are going to need as much brain power and muscle to finish this dome and become self-sustaining," Nicholas added preventing Joe and the Earthlings from initiating a conflict.

The group had been trapped in a spaceship and had awakened to a world unlike the crevice on Ymir that had been developed to satisfy all their human needs. The new dome was a structure waiting to happen, a work in progress, a would-be home for the space travelers. The mood was dark as the group mourned the loss of their second home. Gloom overrode relief in spite of the promise of security and hope for a new community.

Jane rallied the troops with a call to join her and Leia in exploring their new 'digs.' Joyfully, she cried out, "Let's have a party and then the grandparents and aunts and uncles can show Leia that all will be well as soon as we discover the gems of Kepler 452B. This will be her first adventure in our new habitat."

"Splendid idea, Jane," Uncle Ernest yelled out to his neighbors, realizing that gloom and doom was no way to introduce a young generation to a new home in a safety zone.

Only Charles kept the negative ions in the atmosphere, "Let's hope this is the last stop. I am tired of these treks through the universe."

Chapter 32
The Migratory Life

Now that fate has intervened and given us lemons, let's make lemonade," Nicholas told his motley crew of former Ymirians.

"Right on, Commander," Jordan added. We can't let the dreary look of this place get us down. We have made something out of nothing before, and we can do it again."

"...and again and again?" Donald added with a touch of cynicism.

"Yes, yes, if we have to become migrants when our worlds become uninhabitable, we will do it with style and grace. We are a hearty group of living beings who seem to have pushed back on Father Time, survived and thrived. Look, we even have a grandchild to enjoy, and we must protect her." Joshua bellowed in his deepest theatrical voice.

"And we will soon have another grandchild to love and protect," Vicky added as she stood and showed her baby bump protruding from the flexible space suit.

"What?" All the Ymirians gasped.

"Who fathered this child? None of us, except Nicholas, have enough moxie left. Tell us, Vicky,"

Ernest boldly put the question that was on everyone's mind.

"Well, it was not me. I'm a family man, but please respect Vicky's privacy in this matter," Nicholas responded, wanting to kill two birds with one stone as he looked at Jane who was smiling at the thought.

"Thank you, Commander Nicholas, but I am comfortable answering any questions you might have, especially if my friend, Oden, will join me," Vicky said as she reached out her hand to a Gray figure in the crowd.

The Earthling crowd gasped again – some in horror and some in amazement. They were accustomed to change, but this was beyond their capacity to imagine. Calming themselves, they had scattered thoughts. What, when, where? Being humans, they secretly wondered how it had happened but were too embarrassed to ask. The Browns and Grays sighed and ho-hummed since this kind of mating was not at all unknown to them. Variety was the spice of life for their kind.

Oden openly joined Vicky, stood beside her and reached out his limb and grasped her hand. Vicky spoke as the Earthlings listened and read on their pads,

"Oden is the father of my child and will become my partner as we settle into our new home on Kepler. He and I have spent many happy hours communicating and have found that we are simpatico. When I was on Planet Earth, I watched a movie called '*The Shape of Water*' that was a fantasy love story between a creature and a human. The creature was part monster according to some humans but not for Elisa, the heroine. This tale of romance between a river god and a human touched me so much."

"Our paths have crossed, and we have strong feelings or what you call love for each other. Our relationship is not strange to us, and we hope you will accept our union and welcome us as part of the community," Oden wrote as Vicky lovingly looked on while occasionally darting her gaze to the room of listeners.

Silence filled the area where the group had gathered as the Humans struggled to understand. Suddenly, the Browns and Grays stood up in unison and hailed the union on their pads, *"Congratulations, this will be a new era for we former Ymirians as we work towards becoming a truly diversified and progressive culture."*

Jane, the peace maker, stepped forward and embraced both Vicky and Oden, "I could not be happier for you both and know that you will be embraced by us all: and I can't wait to tell Leia that she will have a playmate and companion. She has no partiality to body form given that her experience has been to view differences as the norm."

Gladys was the first to compose herself and comment, "Sweet love has bound you together. I certainly will embrace whomever comes from this union. I also saw that movie, Vicky, and can attest that Del Torro's film challenged my preconceived notions of romance. Of course, in that movie, body forms were similar enough to allow for intimacy. Pardon me, Vicky and Oden; and you don't have to answer if you don't want to, was this a similar process?"

"You do have a no-nonsense way to speak, Gladys. Years of biology training, I suspect," Nicholas added. "Do you want to answer that question or is it none of our business?"

"I will be pleased to answer your question and quell your fears," Oden wrote. *"We Grays have the ability to horizontally pass genetic material via a phage-generated touch. A phage is like a virus. Vicky and I had spoken about this, and she agreed to this when we became committed to each other. There was no coercion or secrecy."*

"Wow," Ara spoke out, "I had learned about this bacterial form of reproduction while in medical school, but I am surprised to learn that it worked in multicellular organisms."

"Ara, this is only one of our many strengths, we have evolved over our lifetimes," Joe added, *"you humans were on a young planet and did not have the advantages of those of us living on older and more evolved worlds in the universe. We have had to develop multiple options to survive."*

"Let's take a breather, Nicholas, I am both physically and emotionally exhausted," Jordan offered to his weary human neighbors who nodded their heads in agreement.

Chapter 33
A Challenge to the Leadership

Jordan had not been able to sleep well following the meeting of the community. He could not get the picture of Vicky and the Gray, Oden, together out of his mind. What would this kind of coupling mean for Homo Sapiens? Was this the end of the species as he knew it? There are more of 'them' than us. Would they take over and overwhelm us with their reproductive power? He could not face the possible reality of a Brown/Gray majority.

When they had left Earth, there had been a big problem with people of color walking across borders to European countries and the Americas. He recalled that the conservative politicians had tried to stop the flow, but the immigrants kept coming and causing turmoil in governments and cultures. The more liberal factions fought to allow for the possible flow of humans into their countries if they were escaping poverty or dangerous conditions to seek asylum once they had been vetted and posed no threat to the safety of the community. Jordan had always believed that people of color would take over the white population and destroy western civilization if these migrants were allowed to enter countries unchecked. This, despite the fact, that everyone agreed that new immigration policies had to be put in place by every country.

He decided to consult with his friend Donald who appeared to agree about the political fallout that had occurred on Earth. He wondered if there were any other worriers in their group. He would begin the conversation with Donald and not Ara who appeared to lean with the more liberal factions in the group.

Jordan tracked down Donald who was roaming around the domed area in search of any sign of water or living organisms.

"Donald, take a break and come and sit with me. I want to discuss an issue of great urgency," Jordan spoke in his usual military curtness.

"So, what is so urgent that you interrupt my business? What could be that important, Dude?" Donald was quick to react to Jordan's tone of voice.

"What did you think of the bombshell Vicky dropped last night?"

Donald stopped his digging and stood up to face Jordan. "Needless to say I was shocked and blind-sided. I had always thought Vicky had a crush on me, not on some odd duck."

"Well, why would she want some old geezer when there is youth and vigor around?" Jordan tried to bring some lightness to the conversation and to incite some animosity and resentment before he brought up the real topic.

"You are right there, old man, but that brings up the question of why Ara would prefer you to the young bucks around on Earth," Donald retorted as they continued to press each other's buttons.

"Good point, but my real concern is this interbreeding between different species. You know that there are many more of them here on Kepler. We are the minority." Jordan began to construct his case.

"Jordan, most of us are too old to breed."

"Remember that scientist on Earth who had genetically engineered mice to give birth to litters at eighty years and above?" Jordan had prepared himself with history and facts.

"Okay, but those were rodents, not humans. What are you proposing, Jordan? Separate the Browns and Grays from our group? Annihilate them? Kill Vicky and the offspring to teach them a lesson?" Donald asked.

"No, these creatures are too valuable to our survival. I have been wondering whether we need new leadership – one who would instill species respect and strict guidelines about fraternizing. In other words, a more military approach to the governance of this community would help to solve the problem or at least slow down what could have devastating effects on white folk." Jordan began to flesh out his plan to the unsuspecting Donald.

"Are you talking about Nicholas's leadership? Do you want to take over and assume power so you can slow down or destroy the amalgamation you predict?" Donald answered while trying to keep calm and composed. He could not believe his ears with the words his old neighbor was saying.

"Ernest and I have been talking about this and think there may be others who will join us in our plan to unseat Nicholas who has shown himself to be too accepting of these kinds of interactions. If we could convince Joe, a more pragmatic leader, to abandon his friendship with Nicholas, we would have a co-captain at the helm," Jordan insisted.

"Nicholas has been a courageous and competent commander who has saved us numerous times. Is this about Vicky and her Gray Oden, Jordan? Are you so fearful of a different species taking us over that you want to become dictator? That reminds me of what was happening on Earth before we left when authoritarian leaders were popping up all over the place in response to the migrations of people in poor or violent countries." Donald pushed back and made his displeasure known to Jordan, the military man.

"This is a question of maintaining our civilization and culture and insuring that our kind will be able to continue to cling to our beliefs," Jordan responded with an increasing ire in the tone of his voice. "I think you have drunk the Kool-Aid, Donald, and you would be a traitor to the cause. Forget I ever brought this up. It probably is an unworkable idea anyway."

"I hope that you mean what you say, Jordan. I will be watching what you and Ernest and any

other member of the cabal are doing to bring conflict and chaos to our community. I can't believe
that Ara knows about this plot." Donald coura-
geously responded to the veiled threat Jordan had
just shared.

"The women in our group don't need to know
anything. Let's not bother their pretty little
heads," Jordan added. "We men can take care of
them as we always have."

Chapter 34
Fateful Intervention?

Despite Donald's watchdog plan, Jordan, Ernest and Charles met to discuss their options and plan a takeover of the leadership. No one suspected, no one mind-read or wondered what the 'men's woodpecker group' was hatching. When asked, the men would say that they wanted to study birds to find a way to bring those creatures to Kepler452B. All of the Ymirians had devoted themselves to building the infrastructure inside the dome and did not bother to check on their neighbors. Members of the secret group joined in the construction as good citizens as they met to flesh out their plan.

While lifting a sheet of plastic wallboard, Jordan fell backwards onto the hard ground and suffered a severe strain in his cervical vertebra. He could not move himself to get up but called out to Donald who was working nearby to help him. Despite Donald's efforts he could not lift Jordan without creating a painful scream that frightened everyone. Others rushed over to help, but Jordan had shouted that no one should touch him. "Call 911," he cried, not realizing that he was not on Planet Earth.

That was the first inkling of the extent of the damage to Jordan's body and mind. Fate had intervened and put an end to the cabal's machinations since Jordan had developed nerve damage in his back extending to his legs in addition to serious problems in his speech and brain, probably a result of a concussion. He had even forgotten his plan to replace Nicholas with himself to bring more separation among the inhabitants of Kepler452B.

In stark contrast to his former beliefs, he allowed the Grays to develop therapy robots who could help him perform his daily chores, and he allowed the Grays to touch him and perform healing acts on his back and legs. Strangely, Oden was one of the first volunteers to visit Jordan each day as Ara had distanced herself from her partner and found many excuses to leave Jordan and work on the building of the dome infrastructure.

No one knew when this placid Jordan would awaken from this dream-like state and revert to his military, misogynistic self. Somehow, he had become someone who had succumbed to the post-apocalyptic syndrome that had affected some of his neighbors who had nightmares and extreme anxieties following the revelation that Earth and all who lived there had been annihilated. Now, his brain had changed to allow for a more mellow fellow. Donald hoped that this new person would remain, allowing the adaptation to take hold in Jordan's brain, forming new connections. Ernest and Charles had seemingly forgotten their reservations about the diversity issues on Kepler452B and their overthrow plan. It was as if it had been erased from their minds.

All was quiet and peaceful while the infrastructure slowly took shape in the hands, arms, appendages and brains of the new inhabitants of this planet that had survived in spite of cataclysmic bombardments from huge space rocks that may have extinguished civilizations gone before. They continued to ask whether there were some survivors still here on Kepler? Were they able to adapt or had they escaped to another home in the Galactic Universe?

Nicholas pondered these questions when he could not sleep. He had read Isaac Asimov's *'Foundation Trilogy'* when he was a youngster and had wondered whether this science fiction could actually exist – societies, some advanced and some neophytes, spread throughout the galaxy. Were the current inhabitants of Kepler452B members of those migratory groups traveling from planet to planet in search of security and safety, doomed to a destiny of intermittent upheaval and space travel.

"I have wondered the same thing," a telepathic Joe communicated to the Commander.

"Geez-us! Can't a guy have a little privacy?" Nicholas responded in a muted voice so as to avoid waking Jane.

"Sorry to disturb you, but I was thinking the same thing, and your thought came through to me. Perhaps you are developing the ability to share

through your consciousness. You know we have been working on ways to make that happen with you Earthlings."

"Another horizontal genetic transmission?" Nicholas responded in an exasperated, cynical tone.

"Anything is possible, Nicholas, but remember that mutations in your genetic makeup could also have occurred in your brain cells and changed the way you communicate. Take the case of Jordan who is now a placid invalid as a result of changes in his brain structure or chemistry, changing from a rigid military man who was planning an overthrow of our leadership just a few months ago."

"What are you talking about, Joe?" Nicholas signaled to his friend and co-pilot. "I was unaware of any such activity."

"Ah yes, it was probably good that you had not gone telepathic, or you would have had to take matters in your human hands. Somehow, fate or some other form of intervention solved the problem," Joe thought, with a shot across the bow to any potential rival who might be thinking of such a move, be it Human, Gray or Brown," *Somehow, fate or some other form of intervention solved the problem."*

Chapter 35
Home Is Where the Heart Is

There was no need to pursue the issue of the failed rebellion. Nicholas knew enough to avoid digging too deeply into the details of the plan or the ensuing consequences because he suspected that Joe had erased the thoughts out of his computer-like brain. Try as he may, Nicholas would not be able to devise a way to retrieve the information from Joe or from the deleted messages in his cache. He decided to move on and to accept the outcome. They should all continue to work together for the good of all regardless of the history of near rebellion.

Nicholas and Joe had taken the trouble to collapse two of the Ymirian engineer/construction robots and store them on the space journey to Kepler452B; and when they decided to awaken the twins, they walked outside the dome and placed them on the terra firma of this planet hoping that the replication process would commence. A rumbling, metallic rustling sound was followed by movement of the materials under the robots who were using the metals on the planet to make copies of themselves. Joe and Nicholas stood in rapt attention as two robots had become an army of hundreds.

"Now we can get down to serious building," Nicholas turned to Joe and sent his thought when he realized that he could communicate with his mind.

"Let's begin by capturing some of that energy from our star in some solar panels to help us develop communication and agriculture." Joe suggested as he had been designing large solar farms during his trip from Ymir.

"Good thinking, Joe, we do know that this planet has plenty of rare earth elements and platinum unlike my former home, Earth, where China held much of those resources. I often wondered why these elements tended to accumulate in certain regions. Hopefully, Kepler452B will have unlimited supplies."

"Unless of course, former inhabitants have mined it to depletion. I suspect that we are not the only space travelers who have lived here or at least used this as a source of raw materials," Joe mused.

Jane joined the duo and reported on her findings, "Greetings from the working stiffs inside the dome. We, by that I mean a group of Browns and Grays and I, have tested the soil here and found that heating via microwaves caused the elements to melt and fuse into ceramic blocks. Now we have some of the building blocks, and all we need is the workforce to construct the structures where we can live, congregate and play."

"Jane, how was I so lucky to have such a brilliant and beautiful partner?" Nicholas walked towards Jane, but Joe intervened by standing between the two figures in space suits and shaking his robe back and forth.

"This is no time for any hanky-panky or emotional displays. We have work to be done," Joe demanded.

"If I didn't know better, I would suspect that you have thoughts or 'feelings' about my Jane. I hope you don't have any horizontal genetic engineering in mind." Nicholas thought without thinking about what he had transmitted.

"Sorry, buddy, I turned off the laser posting so you will never know."

Jane interrupted the locker room thoughts and turned her back on them to walk away as she thought to herself that she had been having some strange feelings during her sleep time. She reminded herself to check her calendar to note the last time she had experienced a period. She would always have vivid sexual dreams about her time with Nicholas, but there was no way she could recall that a robed creature had invaded her thoughts or dreams.

She visited Vicky when she re-entered the maintenance and control part of the dome and asked her about how she knew she was pregnant. Vicky was not much help because this state had been her first, and she had not known what to look for; but she assured Jane that she would had known if one of the Browns or Grays had tried to reproduce with her.

"The feelings were nothing I had ever experienced before while on Earth with any man I had loved. And when I say nothing, I mean NOTHING – a rapture that would last for hours," Vicky swooned.

Jane shared her interaction with Nicholas and Joe earlier in the day and had wanted some re-assurance that Joe had not consulted her before any attempt to mate for fear of Nicholas' re-sponse.

Vicky held out her hand to Jane and spoke in a quiet tone, "Joe would not do anything like that, especially to you; and if he had, you would have known about it, believe me. You know what, Jane? I bet you are pregnant by your Commander, that Earthling, Nicholas."

Jane rushed back to her tent and looked for the calendar. There it was – no period for 2 cycles. She felt somewhat relieved by the finding and cu-rious about Vicky's words, "You would know!"

"That feels like a challenge," she thought as she left to search for her husband to share the good news about the pregnancy and about the rapture she wanted to experience.

Chapter 36
Better Than a Crevice

Under the supervision of Nicholas, Joe, Oden and Brown 1X, the construction of the infrastructure under the dome on Kepler 452B by the hundreds of self-replicating robots had been progressing slowly but carefully. The Browns oversaw the actual construction of the internal structures while the Grays designed and implemented the giant solar panels harvesting solar energy and planning mirrors to orbit their new home to collect sunlight to distribute to the grid they had built.

Those not involved in the design and construction of the dome home provided support and research. The humans would get together each morning to get as much information as they could gather on nanotechnology, terra-farming and laser-porting as processes for the future.

Jane had joined the group and often contributed information from the top brass when she casually communicated to her neighbors, "The work we are doing is going to be very important in the future."

"Why is that, Jane?" Gladys inquired.

"Do you know something we don't but

should?" Donald asked looking squarely in Jane's blue eyes.

"Come on, Jane, what's going on?" Jordan and Ara added in unison.

"I did not mean to alarm you. I was thinking that you were aware that our time on this planet may be limited." Jane offered to get out in front of the discussion.

"You mean that Kepler could be invaded? That atomic warfare could destroy this place, too?" Charles pushed Jane to answer.

"That is only one of the possibilities, folks. This planet could experience extreme heat or cold. The sun, that is in decline, could set the sky on fire once it has exhausted its hydrogen fuel. Planets then could be swallowed in fire as the sun star goes out." Jane continued.

"So our universe could end?" Ernest said. "We would be forced to be on the move again?"

"I think that living beings will have to be ever ready to move to survive or to mutate to insure our existence. We might have to park our bodies somewhere while our consciousness seeks newer, younger, stable universes."

"I was trying to understand that concept as I was researching laser-porting. I find it beyond me that our consciousness could travel as a laser beam and that a living being could become pure energy," Gladys spoke in a soft voice trying to sound as if she understood the conversations swirling around her.

"My, my," Kate added. "If we become pure energy, on top of laser beams, could we bump into each other on that highway?"

That comment broke the foreboding mood of the moment, and all the neighbors broke out in nervous laughter.

"I've been trying to transform this body for as long as I can remember," Joan chuckled and continued, "Diets, dyes, makeup, exercise could be things of the past."

"Would our waves be different? Blondes? Brunettes? Redheads? Fat waves? Skinny Waves?" Vicky added.

"Yeah, would the laser beams travel at different speeds?" Donald cryptically spoke in his usual provocative voice.

The jolly mood was broken when Nicholas and Joe joined the group.

"You are supposed to be working, not having a party. Time is of the essence here. We are going to be ready to move into structures under the dome and test the mechanics and viability of the living condition, but we can't become complacent about the sustainability of this place," Nicholas spoke in his familiar commander tone.

"We had just taken a break from our work and were trying to find some humor in our precarious condition. Come on, Nicholas, cut us some slack. Our feelings of community and comradeship are just as important as the technology we are researching," Jane responded in a scolding wife tone.

Joe interrupted Jane and Nicholas's exchange,

"Nicholas has a point, Jane. "Our lives on this planet are uncertain, and we must begin now to alter ourselves to be able to meet the challenges of the future. We can't wait for random mutations or horizontal genetic transfer as Vicky and Oden have undertaken to give us the characteristics to survive."

"And laser-porting cannot be our only tools. Right now as we still inhabit our bodies, we must utilize computer chips to enhance our brains and muscles and 'Christpit' to alter certain genes that hinder our functioning," Nicholas added.

"It surely sounds as if we will have to change our basic nature and become more like robots until we can fully transition to becoming pure consciousness," Ernest suggested. The listeners began nodding their heads in agreement.

"You have already begun to do that since you are verging on the ability to communicate telepathically with us," Joe added, *"and we Grays have allowed ourselves to resemble parts of Humans and adapt to living in close proximity to Humans and the Browns."*

"And what changes have you made in yourselves? Have you assumed the human form?" Donald pursued the line of questioning initiated by Ernest.

"So far our changes have involved nutritional changes." Joe added. *"Our anatomy has modified to allow for our bodies to process our new diets .We also have mutated to allow us to breathe oxygen in different atmospheres. In addition, we have been studying diverse methods of reproduction that*

would allow for genetic diversity."

"And the Browns, how have they changed or don't engineering types have any interest in modifying themselves?" Jordan asked. "For myself, I am ready to trade in this old body for some newer model or at the very least, genetically enhance my muscles and nerves."

"You want to be younger and stronger to keep up with your younger partner, right?" Donald responded while poking Jordan in the arm. "I do recall that Earth scientists had succeeded in genetically modifying mice to make them into 'Mighty Mice' who could run faster and live longer than their normal selves. They could even reproduce in old age."

"Let's stay on topic, folks," Nicholas said in his firm commander-like voice.

"We are a very basic planetary civilization in that we have learned to use solar power instead of the fossil fuels or fusion power used on your earth. We are now building vast mirrors to collect sunlight energy. These are bigger and more powerful than the ones we use now," Joe continued.

"But we can't depend on these suns to last forever nor can we avoid the heating of Kepler452B from these powerful mirrors capturing the solar energy. We have to find other sources of energy from our galaxy or at some point from other galaxies, and that means we have to prepare ourselves and our progeny to be able to move from planet to planet if Kepler heats up," Nicholas added to Joe's narrative.

"This sounds all so hypothetical. These changes could or could not happen, right? Do we have a vote as a community or do we have to accept these views as fact?" Donald asked the leaders in his role of acting as a spokesperson for the group.

Jordan added his voice to Donald's as he seemed to have awoken from his peaceful, submissive self to become a fomenter of dissent, "What evidence do you have to support your ideas of Armageddon in our galaxy or the burning of Kepler?"

"Hear, hear" Donald shouted out to the crowd. "Remember what Mark Twain said about science – science gets a lot of return on conjecture out of a trifling number of facts."

"Donald, astronomy and physics rely on some elusive time machine detection and measurements of light waves as seen through telescopes, but their mathematical calculations confirm some of their basic ideas concerning the life of certain planets. Much about the death of the universe is conjecture based on hypotheses put forward by scientists who have spent their lives studying. No, there is not an experiment that proves that our sun may burn out, but it seems prudent to conclude that we are better off accepting their hypotheses and planning for a different future than ignoring their findings.

"We must visualize landscapes of possible universes where we could find a young one that is stable and might contain billions of galaxies. We could then look for planets to inhabit." Nicholas responded as he attempted to acknowledge their concerns without giving up authority.

"We may be required to live in multiverses," Jane added. "It isn't what I imagined, but we must face reality."

"This sounded like the controversy about climate change that occurred on Earth. The scientists provided their observations and algorithms while the deniers saw economic disaster and inadequate evidence that humans could influence the climate," Gladys added.

"That happened to our home, too. The controversy unleashed a fierce battle between the opposing sides that led to a war of extinction." A member of the Browns wrote and translated for the Humans and the Grays. The other members of the Browns added to the communication via telepathy to confirm the original message.

Vicky and Oden stood up in the back of the gathering area and shared their dreams about having their child live in safety on any planet that could sustain life. "I don't care how many times we move or in whatever form we assume as long as we can be together," Vicky offered as she leaned into her Oden.

Joshua entered the fray and with the voice of a Julius Caesar, said, "I don't see where we have much choice but to listen to what Nicholas and Joe have to say since they are the scientists and technologists among us. I am a lowly actor and can put on a good face; but in reality, I am gripped in fear of our future. I see a bright cloud in these warnings – that we won't perish from disease or the Grim Reaper if we prepare for the worst. We will be able to continue to roam around the galaxies in different forms but with the same core. True or False?"

"As far as we know, Joshua! Even in science, we find no guarantees." Joe responded. *"So tell us, Keplerians, are we in this together?"*

"Let's dare to dream and get to work to prepare for an uncertain future. Better safe than sorry," Nicholas shouted as he watched the hands, the brown and gray appendages emerging from the cloaks, and the multitude of positive, affirming thoughts coming his way.

"I guess life as we know it, is a journey and not a home," Joan chuckled.

"And it isn't a destination either, but we have learned that uncertainty can bring about many possibilities. Let's accept the things we cannot change but work like hell to change the things we can," Gladys added as they lifted their eyes towards the starry sky and resigned themselves to an uncertain future.

About the Author

Gloria Hanson has been writing poetry and essays since she was in grade school. As a bookworm and curious teenager, she would indulge in flights of fancy during those long after school hours without television or computer. Following a short career in Biology and a long job as wife and mother, she returned to graduate school to study clinical social work. During her professional life she devoted herself to writing articles in her field.

With the departure of children for their own lives, Gloria returned to her early love affair with writing. Now the passion consumes most of her days, resulting in the publication of six books.

This book, **seeking...** is an attempt by the author to write a predictive allegory in a science fiction format. The current advances in astronomy and the beautiful photographs of our expanding universe have fascinated Gloria and piqued her imagination. This book is an endeavor to combine the world around her and the world beyond her.